"No, Cadence— I won't have it!"

He was actually shaking her. "It's Christopher you love. It has to be. You can't do this—to me, to Christopher."

Between tears and laughter, she said, "Oh, Jon, there's nothing you can do about it. I love you. I can't help it, and I don't know what to do."

"It's not true. You've got to love Christopher." Jon's hands dropped to her waist, instinctively drawing her body up close against his. "I always knew you were dangerous—you'll destroy us all."

"Do you think I haven't spent days thinking that? I do understand, but—" She broke off, overwhelmed by the tragic impossibility of their situation and convulsed at the same time by a spasm of pure physical need. "Love me, Jon..."

His face was agonized, his mouth harsh as it descended to hers....

JAYNE BAULING wrote for years before she found the
confidence to let anyone see what she was doing. Now
she writes full-time. But she still finds time to putter in her
large untidy garden and breed sealpoint cats. Traveling,
she says, is her obsession—so for her, real-life romance is
often necessarily a long-distance affair.

Books by Jayne Bauling

HARLEQUIN PRESENTS

These books may be available at your local bookseller.

Don't miss any of our special offers. Write to us at the
following address for information on our newest releases.

Harlequin Reader Service
901 Fuhrmann Blvd., P.O. Box 1397, Buffalo, NY 14240
Canadian address: P.O. Box 603,
Fort Erie, Ont. L2A 9Z9

JAYNE BAULING

abode of princes

Harlequin Books

TORONTO • NEW YORK • LONDON
AMSTERDAM • PARIS • SYDNEY • HAMBURG
STOCKHOLM • ATHENS • TOKYO • MILAN

Harlequin Presents first edition November 1986
ISBN 0-373-10928-8

Original hardcover edition published in 1986
by Mills & Boon Limited

CHAPTER ONE

THE aircraft was just beginning its descent as Cadence Reay made her way back to her seat. Her newly applied make-up was too light to mask the glow of health and happiness that came from within, and beneath the simple cream skirt her bare brown legs were long and slender enough to draw the eyes of the several men occupying aisle seats.

She would never have described herself as beautiful, but her twenty-two years had been packed with sufficient fortune and friends to instil the sort of self-assurance that gave a swing to her step, and it was her general air of well-being and fearless confidence that people of both sexes found so attractive.

Seating herself next to the still drowsy Christopher, she looked at him lovingly, then past him to see if Bombay was in view yet, and finally at the brilliant ring that blazed on her left hand, white and yellow diamonds in a setting that was unique because it had been exclusively designed.

She drew a quick, delighted breath and held it, hardly able to control the effervescence of her mood, and her honey-amber eyes sparkled. She was excited and she didn't care who knew it. Cadence never made a secret of her feelings and she saw no point in pretending to be blasé about the adventure that lay ahead.

Life was wonderful, Christopher was wonderful, and now, most wonderful of all, they were about to land in India, surely the most exciting country in the world.

She turned her bright head to smile at her fiancé,

who was watching the play of her emotions with indulgent affection.

'You're sure Jon will be there to meet us?'

'Of course.' Christopher laughed. 'He'd better be!'

She saw the absolute certainty in the clear grey eyes with just the hint of soft blue in their depths, and with a sudden uprush of protective love thought emphatically that she would rather die than let anyone hurt him. Christopher was sensitive and trusting, and he admired Jon Steele far too much.

Jon Steele. He was Christopher's best friend and as close as a brother, having been brought up by the Iversons since the age of ten. He was also, as far as Cadence was concerned, the only drawback to this Indian trip.

Cadence was a cinema-addict and when she was younger there had been a fashion for what she thought of as buddy-buddy movies. She had always found herself faintly riled by the comparative unimportance of the women in the lives of the various macho protagonists who indulged in supposedly manly pursuits, saved each other's lives and generally made heroic sacrifices in the name of friendship.

A faint smile returned to her lips as she acknowledged that it was probably plain jealousy which was causing her to view Jon Steele as the single flaw in an otherwise perfect pattern. Until Christopher had met her, Jon had been the most important person in his life, and it occurred to her to wonder if Jon was also feeling a similar resentment.

Cadence's face was carved in utterly feminine lines, cleanly but delicately sculpted to give an impression of indivisible strength and fragility, those two conflicting qualities that made the female truly a woman. Now her jaw tightened resolutely.

Christopher was all that mattered. For his sake, she

was determined to like Jon Steele, to get on with him, and if he was the man Christopher and his parents believed him to be, Jon would have made a similar resolve, knowing how much it meant to Christopher. For Christopher's sake, they would both make an effort.

She relaxed. There was nothing to worry about. Problems, difficulties—they afflicted other people, but she, by some blessed chance, travelled a smooth road. She was the luckiest girl in the world and properly appreciative of it, occasionally wondering if there really was such a thing as being born under a lucky star.

It was going to be absolutely perfect, this holiday in India.

'You won't have any business meetings scheduled for today, will you?' she questioned Christopher, remembering that it wasn't purely pleasure that had brought them to India.

'No, thank God.'

'I can't wait to hit the streets!' she exclaimed happily. 'Bombay! Just think, Christopher!'

He was laughing gently at her enthusiasm. 'Then you'd better have a word with Jon and he can show you around. All I can think of is a shower and then bed for the next few hours.'

'Oh, come on!' she teased, resting her smooth cheek on his shoulder. 'You're never tired? I feel full of energy!'

'You always do! Just remember, my love, that I'm eight years older than you——'

'Poor old Grandpa!'

'And it's not yet four-thirty in the morning, Bombay-time, and we've been sitting in this plane for—how many hours?' he continued, dropping a kiss on her head. 'But I'm sure Jon will be delighted to escort you, and it will be a chance for you to get to know each other.'

It meant so much to him, Cadence reflected. He really wanted his friend and his fiancée to like each other, and of course she hoped his expectations would be fulfilled. Otherwise—well, she could always start exploring Bombay on her own, although Christopher seemed to think that she needed an escort. She would be careful, of course. His stories about his own first visit to India, also for Iverson Travel, when he was a gullible young man still learning the business, had made her laugh, but they had also made her realise that the vast subcontinent was utterly different from the countries she was accustomed to, and until now Germany was the farthest she had ever been away from home.

She sat up straight as the call came to fasten seatbelts, glancing at Christopher and hoping fervently that the reunion with his friend would prove to be all he expected. Of course it would be, just as long as Jon Steele approved of her, and how he and she reacted to each other lay with the gods—and with themselves, she supplemented with the serene conviction that where any small obstacle lay in the road, a little extra personal effort would certainly eliminate it.

And Christopher Iverson merited any amount of effort. Cadence's eyes travelled over his long, lean frame and handsome fair head. She was so lucky to have met him, to be loved by him, because—oh, she loved him so very much.

She had been in love any number of times before meeting him. Coming as she did from a close, loving family in which she was the younger sister of two brothers, a constant stream of boys and later men had featured in her life. Many of her best friends were male and many of her boy-friends had remained friends after it was all over. She had regarded the end of each new romantic interest with philosophical acceptance rather than with bitter disappointment as she was young and in no hurry to meet the great love of her life, thanks in part to her own personality and partly to a sensible upbringing.

She had been learning about herself and it had seemed to her that generally the men who attracted her physically provided her with little in the way of emotional or intellectual stimulation, whereas those whom she liked and found entertaining were also those with whom she could never imagine herself sharing the intimacies of a physical relationship.

In Christopher, she considered, she had found the perfect whole. She liked and respected him, and she also loved him enough to want to be his wife and share his bed and have his children. The fact that they had not yet become lovers in the full sense caused her little concern. She was still young and still in no hurry, and Christopher could be waiting until they were married, as he had a few endearingly old-fashioned ideas about gentlemanly behaviour inherited from his darling of a father, although Cadence suspected that it might happen this holiday now that they both had time and freedom at their disposal. They had been so busy up until now, their lives governed by the demands of their different positions in Iverson Travel.

Cadence had worked for the company ever since completing a travel agent's course on leaving school, gradual promotions over the years having brought her to the stage where she was in charge of the small branch in the main shopping centre of the pleasant, moderately comfortable London suburb in which she had grown up. She had had no desire for a transfer since she could continue living at home, paying nominal board, and thus save more towards her own modest travels in Europe.

Six months ago, she had met Christopher Iverson, the son and heir, when the heads of all agencies had been required to attend a cocktail party and film show detailing a new line in camping holidays for the young.

She hadn't been the only girl looking at him that evening, but she had been the only one at whom he was looking, and—that had been that! Both families had been delighted, everyone liked everyone else, and it only remained for Cadence to be introduced to the absent Jon Steele who was so important to all the Iversons.

Christopher and his parents had talked about Jon right from the start, the man Christopher looked up to as he would to an older brother, for Jon was the senior by five years. Cadence knew every adventure of their boyhood, every escapade of their teens. She had looked at photos of a man as dark as Christopher was fair, and listened enthralled to tales of the wild exploits of their young manhood. She had even, a little reluctantly, read the books the family had proudly pressed on her, books by Jon Steele that were simply written accounts of those exploits, direct, almost tersely understated chronicles of adventures in the Himalayas, the Antarctic, along the Amazon, on an overland trip through African desert and jungle, and similar projects, which were yet ultimately gripping and remained vivid in her mind long after she had closed the books.

Finally she had come to the conclusion that Jon led and Christopher followed—out of loyalty, because she was sure he wasn't as naturally reckless as Jon seemed to be. Christopher had his own brand of wanderlust and worldwide vision, as had his father, who had broken away from a family tradition in the Church of

England to found Iverson Travel, beginning with one small office and expanding into the concern it was today with agencies throughout Britain and a reputation as good as any. But Jon Steele's restlessness was something else again and, reading his books, Cadence had shuddered, convinced that it had been shot through with a death wish.

Of course, his later books were calmer in content, more about the peoples of the places he roamed, as if the frets and fevers of the young man had burned themselves out and his need to wander the world had become more cerebral and less physical, but he still came across as a hard man with no illusions, and she supposed that was why he never wrote fiction. How he and her gentle Christopher could have anything in common was beyond guessing.

From Christopher, and from Aubrey and Stephanie, as his parents had urged her to call them, she had gleaned bits of information about Jon Steele's strange story until she had been able to piece together his history. There was much there, she had to admit, to have caused wildness in youth and hardness in maturity, yet it was the one story he had never written.

He had been born in the country in which they were about to land, not very many years after Independence, but the family of three had moved on soon afterwards, in obedience to the whim of the father, an explorer frustrated by the fact that there was so little left of the world to explore and whose self-indulgent eccentricity was only matched by the shrewdness with which he invested his wealth, a talent inherited by his son. At five, Jon Steele had seen his mother washed away by an African river in flood. At ten, in India once more, he had lost his father to an elephant in must, an appropriately violent end for a man who had courted danger all his life.

The orphaned son had then proceeded to lose himself among India's millions.

'He ran away,' Stephanie Iverson had explained to Cadence. 'I don't know what was in his mind, and he never told us afterwards. Thank God it was in India and not one of the really uncivilised places they so often travelled to. Even so, it took months to find him, and he's never explained how he lived except to say that he kept on the move. Think of it! A child who had just inherited a massive fortune, and everyone looking for him. Aubrey had been at school with his father, but they'd lost touch after the mother's death, so he was pretty surprised to find that he'd been named as Jon's guardian. He went out to fetch the boy when he was finally apprehended, having made his way to Delhi, and I just quailed when I saw what he'd brought back with him, a wild, bitter boy with a man's eyes, lashing out at everyone, insisting he didn't need anyone or anything, a mocking, sarcastic young misanthropist . . . My son was five at the time and I was dreading the effect this young savage would have on him, but the strangest thing happened the first time they met. Christopher was at that age to admire any bigger boy, and he took one look at Jon and decided this was going to be his hero. I forget what he said— something so innocent—he was still only a baby really, and I just wanted to pick him up and carry him off out of harm's way because I could literally see some cutting retort forming on Jon's lips, and my baby had never met with rejection before . . . But Cadence, Jon never said it. I was watching him and I saw the anger die in his eyes. He didn't say anything then, just shrugged and turned away, but that was the beginning. I've never been able to explain it.'

'It was Christopher,' Cadence had claimed with loving pride. 'He's special, and people recognise that—even savages like the boy you've described. Nobody could ever hurt Christopher.'

'He does seem to invite only goodwill, and without even trying,' Christopher's mother conceded smilingly. 'Anyway, that's the way it's been ever since. Jon may have led Christopher into a few rash escapades in their time, but he was always careful to ensure that no real harm or hurt came to him, and gradually that attitude was extended to Aubrey and me as well. Quite as much as he was a brother to Christopher, he became a son to us. It had been a sadness when we discovered that I couldn't have any more children, and Jon filled the gap. He's one of the family and we love him and he loves us. That's why, when he undertook all those mad ventures of his, I was glad that he'd Christopher with him. Alone, he might have taken terrible risks, but he would never let Christopher come to any harm. Keeping Christopher safe, he was being kept safe by Christopher, if you see what I mean.'

Cadence had refrained from comment, knowing that hearsay alone was no basis on which to form judgements, but she often thought about Jon Steele's importance in the lives of the Iversons. Stephanie had claimed that he returned their love, but Cadence sometimes wondered if the man who had written those books was capable of loving. She hoped at the least that he appreciated the warm, wonderful family who had shared their lives with him and tolerated his wild ways.

Their loving regard for him amounted almost to adoration. They talked about him constantly and it was a matter of some importance to Christopher that Jon and Cadence should meet and like each other.

Which was why they were about to land in Bombay.

Iverson Travel were conscientious and proud of their reputation. Nothing was delegated; the personal touch was their motto and the directors themselves made frequent trips to every country in the world to which they offered tours, assessing and reassessing the accommodation they selected for their clients, mercilessly discarding any establishment where there was a decline in the standards for which it had originally been chosen, and setting an equally high standard for the local guides they employed. As an influential member of the board, Christopher had had little difficulty in wangling this Indian trip, and Cadence had been granted extended leave, partly due to her future position in the Iverson family, but also because she was due to sit one of Iverson Travel's internal exams when they returned which, if she passed, would mean being transferred to the London head office and promotion to the position of tour co-ordinator.

She would miss dealing direct with the public, she knew, but it meant she and Christopher would be working in the same building. Anyway, once they started their family, they had agreed that she would stop work, since money would never be one of their worries.

They had everything going for them, and they both knew it. They were young, in love, and their wedding was set for next April. There had never been any question of its taking place earlier than that because Jon Steele was adamant in refusing to cut short the year he was allowing himself in India and Christopher couldn't contemplate anyone else as his best man.

An April wedding, then, followed by a honeymoon which would be necessarily short to compensate for these six weeks in India, but again Cadence reflected that this would probably turn out to be the real honeymoon. She had even been to her doctor to obtain the requisite protection, since they had no intention of starting their family for another eighteen months to two years.

Every detail was beautifully planned, right down to the fact that Jon Steele would be asked to be godfather to their first child.

There was a slight bump as they touched down on the runway and Cadence craned round Christopher to see what was visible in the breaking early morning light, but it wasn't much, so she took his hand and asked:

'Why was Jon so positive about not curtailing this year he's allowing himself in India?'

Laughing, Christopher linked his fingers with hers. 'Who knows? This is a major and comprehensive work he's engaged in, or it could be the fatal fascination of India—and believe me, that's no myth. Or it could be a woman.'

'He's attractive to women?'

'Cady, my love?' He widened his eyes incredulously. 'You've seen the man's photos?'

'And all I saw was a man!'

'You'll know when you meet him. But is it worrying you? He seems to be on your mind. You're not nervous, are you?'

'No, but I just keep remembering that it's due to him that we can't get married until April. He's very important to you and your parents, I know, and I don't quite understand why.'

'You'll understand when you meet him,' Christopher reiterated.

'I wish we were married already.' Cadence always said what she felt.

'So do I!'

Heedless of any of their fellow-passengers who might be watching, Christopher leaned forward and round to kiss her on the mouth, and once again

Cadence thought how lucky she was. Christopher wasn't just her fiancé and future lover and husband; he was also her best friend in all the world.

'I feel I ought to do as the Pope does and kneel and kiss the ground,' she was telling him whimsically not many minutes later as she set foot in India for the first time in her young life.

Eyes alight with love and laughter, Christopher flung his free arm about her. 'I do love you, darling— your enthusiasm for everything! Kiss the ground if you like—it won't cause any stir. This is India, and anything goes.'

'I'll kiss you instead!' She did so, enjoying being told of his love. 'I know I'm talking too much, but I'm just so excited, you see. This is India, Christo, this is It!'

And once the meeting with Jon Steele was over, she knew, she was going to enjoy every minute of their six weeks.

She was enjoying it already, in fact. Bombay's airport at four-thirty in the morning was probably no less chaotic than at any other time of day, a furore of sound and colour. A Gulf Air flight had landed just before theirs, and Air Mauritius and Alitalia followed close on their heels. Passport Control was a simple affair but, after collecting their luggage, Customs proved a different matter.

In love with several dozen people already, even those who kept spitting, and assorted officials, aggressive, courteous, shy or plain bored, Cadence kept turning round to absorb new scenes. She only wondered how many hours it would take them to get through when the homecoming Indians from the Gulf Air flight had apparently brought with them every conceivable household requisite from great rolls of carpets and boxes of stereo equipment to every convenience the modern housewife could possibly require in her kitchen.

But Christopher wasn't ashamed to mention the Iverson connection, and suddenly a short plump man in uniform was waving them through with their luggage and exchanging pleasantries with Christopher as he signed a declaration, while Cadence scanned the waiting crowds.

She saw Jon Steele before he saw them.

She wanted to turn to Christopher and say, 'Look, there he is!' But she could not, frozen in the moment of her comprehension, unable to speak or move as she finally understood why this man meant so much to the Iversons.

The photos she had looked at suddenly seemed travesties, wan imitations of the man. Never in her life had she seen anyone so vibrantly alive. He stood utterly still as he spoke to the girl at his side whose dress proclaimed her a Muslim in this country Cadence had naïvely assumed to be Hindu, and yet his sheer masculine beauty and his energy, a sort of animal vitality, seemed to strike her like a blow, stealing the breath from her lungs and causing her stomach to lurch as if she were on a rollercoaster.

He stopped talking to the girl and looked up, eyes bluer than any sea or sky she had ever seen, scanning the crowds, sweeping over her and on, and then returning to her.

For the first time in her life, Cadence felt a need to dissemble. Guilt and fear, the root causes of untruth, were unknown to her, but she pretended to be heedless of his arrested attention and turned, smiling, to Christopher, who was moving to join her.

'Where in all this crowd is Jon? Can you see him?' She sounded oddly breathless.

She was lying, to Christopher Iverson and to Jon Steele.

My God! she thought. Her thoughts were wild, crazy, without any sense at all. Once seen, never forgotten! No wonder, no wonder . . .

'No—yes! There he is!'

He strode forward and Cadence followed, her thoughts running on hysterically, although she was beginning to recover a little and was even able to be amused by herself, the two men—the entire situation.

At least they didn't embrace! But then they didn't in the buddy-buddy movies either, or not until one of the buddies either lay dying or had just performed some nerve-racking and pointless feat supposedly aimed at proving he was a man.

'I don't need to introduce you two, do I?' Christopher was turning to Cadence, drawing her forward and giving her a gentle little push in Jon Steele's direction.

Jon was laughing, blazing blue eyes brilliant with a sardonic amusement which Cadence instinctively distrusted.

'Do I have to wait for the wedding to kiss the bride?'

He didn't wait for Christopher's silent, smiling permission either, but dropped his hands to Cadence's shoulders and bent his dark head to touch cool lips to her firm, tanned cheek.

Briefly, Cadence did battle with an inexplicable sense of outrage, conquered it and forced a tight, bright smile. For Christopher's sake, she kissed him back and found it strange that her lips should burn and tingle when she had been scrupulously careful to make the salute the merest touch on his hard jaw.

Christopher said teasingly, 'Actually, Cadence was just reminding me that she would be a bride already if you had been prepared to make a trip home before April.'

Jon turned his scintillating gaze on Cadence once more. 'Are you very cross with me, sweetheart? Formalities are important to you?'

She loathed the slight taunting note there, but obviously Christopher hadn't detected it since he was still smiling happily.

'Who doesn't enjoy a good wedding?' she challenged airily. 'And Christopher's and mine is going to be the best you've ever seen! But I'll forgive you, Jon. I'm sure your reasons are . . . worthy.'

For the life of her, she could not prevent a look in the direction of the Muslim girl, who was about her own age, wondering if she could be the woman about whom Christopher had hypothesised earlier.

Jon Steele saw the glance and his lips quirked, but he made no comment, merely drawing the girl into their little group and introducing her as Jahanara Khan.

'My invaluable assistant, whose brother has generously allowed her to come to Bombay for these few days.'

That was her answer, Cadence realised, meeting his eyes and inclining her head very slightly, the tiniest of movements, signalling her understanding. Very subtly, he was warning her that things were different in India. Jahanara Khan might enjoy a degree of freedom that would have shocked her forebears, but there were limits to it, rigid and inviolable.

'I would need a long engagement myself,' Jahanara referred to the earlier exchange. 'There's so much to do, to prepare. It must be very exciting. Do you have a ring? May I see?'

Delighted to show it off, Cadence held out her slim capable hand, moving it from side to side so that the facets of the diamonds caught the light, and she and Jahanara both gazed at the scintillating stones with the romantic reverence women the world over feel for beautiful jewellery, especially when it symbolises the love between men and women.

'I do love jewellery,' Jahanara sighed rapturously, sweeping back her glossy black hair and caressing one of her own earrings, a small ruby encircled by tiny diamonds. 'Congratulations, Cadence ... Oh, no! That's wrong, isn't it? The man is congratulated. Congratulations, Mr Iverson.'

'Christopher, and thank you.' He returned her shy smile kindly.

'Oh, I think they're both to be congratulated, Jahanara,' Jon asserted, the faintest of drawls causing Cadence to look at him sharply. 'Who chose it?'

He had picked up her left hand in his right, and she fought an impulse to snatch it away from him, forcing herself to stand calmly and wear a smile as he examined the ring, and all the while she felt as if a thousand frantic butterflies inhabited her stomach, and an irrational resentment welled up in her, making her eyes flash angrily—because he was holding her hand, marking her, and she would never be free of his touch again.

Dear God, her fingers were actually trembling against the hardness of his. Did he know?

'We both did,' Christopher answered his question. 'We discussed what we wanted and then told the jeweller, and his designer added a few improvements we hadn't thought of.'

'You've shown your usual good taste—and your usual good taste,' Jon repeated, eyes coming to rest on Cadence's suntanned face. 'She's very lovely, Christopher, and I wish you both all the happiness in the world.'

Cadence's heart lurched at the words and her throat tightened emotionally as she witnessed Christopher's smile of pure contentment and the calm radiance that came to his beloved eyes as he received his friend's blessing.

Shakily, she withdrew her fingers from Jon's light clasp, more disconcerted by his smile now, when only sincerity lay behind it, than she had been while suspecting him of some sort of subtle mockery.

'She's also very nice, Jon,' Christopher added quietly. 'Intelligent and kind and wise and bright——'

'You're embarrassing me, Christo!' laughed Cadence, moving to his side and curling her arm about his, gripped by a sudden need to reassure herself of his reality. 'Let's leave Jon to find out for himself and hope that he comes to the same conclusion.'

'I'm sure I will,' Jon said smoothly, and yet there was something else there, as if he hoped otherwise, but only Cadence, alert to every nuance of voice and look, seemed to detect it. 'Shall we go? The car isn't far away. Jahanara and I flew to Bombay, so I hired it on arrival yesterday morning. Jahanara, will you look after Cadence, while Christopher and I deal with the luggage? Take the keys, and be careful. We don't want to lose her.'

And even that, so lightly said, seemed to carry an additional meaning for Cadence in her hypersensitive state. She cast him a last contemplative look before hastening to obey Jahanara's injunction to stay close behind her, and she thought——

Does he know? Oh, dear God, does he know?

Christopher didn't know, obviously, but Jon? Then she thought—what was there to know? She didn't know herself, she didn't understand anything.

'I just can't believe this,' she muttered with an angry laugh, and Jahanara probably thought she was referring to the press of humanity all about them through which she was boring a way with the combined dexterity and force that mark a long experience of India.

Cadence could only follow or be swept away. The situation was out of her control—everything was out of her control!

CHAPTER TWO

OUTSIDE the airport building, Cadence understood Jon's injunction to Jahanara more clearly. The crowds were even denser here, supplemented by a fair number of mostly youthful beggars, while other forms lay sleeping on this and opposite pavements, apparently undisturbed by the masses about them, although a few were in the process of waking to face another day in India.

'India's teeming millions,' Cadence quoted with the return of some of her earlier excitement since she had never seen anything like it before, and Jahanara giggled.

'Hardly millions, but it gets better. Watch your bag——' She broke off to administer a sharp rebuke to one small urchin who kept dodging persistently in front of her.

'I thought the secret was not to make eye-contact?'

'That's for you.'

'Me?'

'You all.' Jahanara giggled again. 'My brother would be shocked if he knew what I said to that boy! Here's the car, Cadence. Get in and we'll wait for the men. Shall we take the back seat?'

It was not yet properly light, but the humidity of the early September morning was intense. Cadence slid into the seat with a sigh of relief and Jahanara followed her.

'I'm just so excited to be here, I can't begin to tell you!' Cadence confided breathlessly, her natural resilience beginning to reassert itself after the shock of meeting Jon Steele and her first encounter with India.

'And we're excited to have you. You must make the most of Bombay, you and Mr Iverson.'

'Yes, it's a pity we've only got two days here before we move on.'

'Ah, but you'll love Rajasthan.'

'It's your home?'

'Yes.'

'I thought it was . . . I'm sorry, weren't they mostly Hindu? The royal clans there and their people?'

'Ah, but back in the very old days, centuries ago, my people were always invading, winning and losing and winning again, making alliances, breaking them . . . My own family has been there longer than our personal records show, in a modest way to begin with and gradually prospering, and not even Partition could change that. India is our country, Rajasthan our state. Do you know that India has the second largest Muslim population in the world? Here are the men. Keys, Jon!' She handed them through the window, assured herself that she couldn't be overheard, and went on, 'He's very handsome, your Mr Iverson, so very fair. His skin is paler than yours, though not much. Some of my friends don't like the European looks, but I think they are romantic.'

'So do I, Jahanara, so do I!' laughed Cadence. 'Especially Christopher's.'

'Christopher. It's a nice name,' Jahanara commented, so dreamily that Cadence wondered if she was developing a crush on Christopher, but she was too tactful to tease. Clearly, Jahanara was of a deeply romantic disposition.

The men got into the front of the car, laughing in a way that indicated man-talk, and she wondered if they had been doing as Jahanara had and discussing the opposite sex. Probably. Was there any subject of greater interest to either sex?

She was glad Christopher was happy. She must take care not to be possessive, to give him time alone with his friend. After all, the two of them went back a long way, and those undercurrents she had discerned in Jon's speech could merely mean that he was jealous of her new importance in Christopher's life.

Only wasn't jealousy a rather petty, if altogether human, emotion? And Jon Steele didn't strike her as either petty or human. What acquaintance had he with emotion of any sort, either petty or grand? Did he love, hate, hunger? Or did he just exist?

At least he cared about Christopher. Well, he hadn't said anything to distress him yet, and he could so easily have done. Being in love made people silly, it made her and Christopher silly, but Jon had refrained from making any taunting comment.

Therefore he was kind to Christopher. That, as far as Cadence was concerned, was his saving grace.

Because she didn't like Jon Steele, she concluded, deciding that her earlier reaction had probably been either imagination or a combination of fatigue, heat, jet-lag and the India shock. Plain dislike was easier to handle, and just too bad, but for Christopher's sake, she would work at it, discover Jon's good points and make herself like him.

She stared at Jon's back which was directly in front of her since he was driving. Dark hair, almost black, strong suntanned neck, powerful but graceful shoulders under a good, simple shirt . . . She felt her mouth dry and her stomach flip.

Well, damn it, Cadence thought furiously, angry with both Jon and herself. He was too sexy and she was probably oversexed. She wasn't a child, she knew what lust was, didn't she? It never meant anything, because that was an area in which familiarity definitely bred contempt. A few hours ago, hadn't she been thinking one of the cabin stewards was dead sexy? Being in love with Christopher didn't mean she had lost her ability to appreciate the more magnificent specimens of the male sex, but she couldn't even clearly remember what that steward had looked like now. Lust was something that happened in your loins, but never in your brain or your heart, and it was ephemeral and fickle. Lust was what she felt sometimes in her personal life, experienced occasionally when she went to the cinema and knew regularly every Wimbledon fortnight as she followed the fortunes of various athletic Americans, tanned Australians, black-haired South Americans and blond-locked Swedes.

Only! She stared at the back of Jon's head, admiring the way his hair was cut. She had never for a moment wondered or cared what was going on inside the minds of those tennis players and the others, but the contents of that well-shaped skull in front of her were of the most profound interest. She would dearly love to know what he was thinking—and feeling!

She transferred her gaze to Christopher's fair head, then to Jahanara and finally back to Jon. What was wrong with her? All right, it must be jet-lag and she was light-headed with it. Did you suffer from it coming from west to east, or was it only the other way? She couldn't remember. She ought to have gone on one of those special anti-jet-lag diets beforehand, like President Reagan when he went to China; then she wouldn't be feeling like this, knocked off balance and desperately unsure of herself for the first time in her life.

'Jon! Jon?' There was a pause in the conversation that had flowed between the two men, and Jahanara spoke anxiously from beside Cadence. 'Shouldn't we warn Cadence and Christopher about this drive from the airport? I should hate to have them judge Bombay by what we're seeing now and spend the next two days in the hotel.'

Surprised to discover she had been concentrating more on Jon than on the India outside, Cadence immediately looked out of the windows, turning her head from side to side, anxious not to miss anything. She supposed the grey, rather squalid blocks of flats would be called slums at home, but more intriguing by far were the people who slumbered on the hard pavements, casually, confidently, and the taxi drivers sprawled on the bonnets of their cars sleeping while they waited for the fares that morning would bring.

'Relax, Jahanara,' Jon advised. 'Christopher has been to India before, and I'm sure he's warned Cadence.'

'That, in common with so many other cities all around the world, the first impression is the worst if you come by air.' Cadence's smile was wide and warm until she met Jon's vivid eyes in the rearview mirror when it became a forced, frozen grimace. 'But so far, this looks like the country for me. I can also sleep anywhere.'

'Yes,' Christopher agreed darkly. 'She slept like a baby in its mother's arms all the way over while I fretted and fumed and kept waking. That's why she's raring to be up and off, investigating Bombay's darkest secrets, while all I can think of is bed! Jon, are you feeling gallant? Because if Cady wants to be out and about, I'm not going to sleep unless I know someone is with her.'

Jahanara leaned towards Cadence, whispering, 'He has such a care for you, so considerate, so protective. You must feel privileged . . . pampered!'

'Oh, I do!' Cadence stopped smiling as she met Jon's enigmatic blue eyes in the rearview mirror again. 'Well, Jon, what do you say? Can Christo sleep?'

'It rests with you, lady. If you want to see the sights, I'm your man for a few hours, but if it's shopping you want—speak to Jahanara. She's the most dedicated and professional shopper I've ever met. It's an art form with her, and a matter of pride. She knows every trick!'

Mirrored eyes met once more, the dark honey pair limpidly innocent. 'I want both, but I think I'll go for the sight-seeing first. If that suits you, Jon? As Christopher said earlier, it will be a chance for us to get to know each other, and I'd like that . . . Wouldn't you?'

She was unsure if it was a challenge she issued or whether she was motivated by the need to talk to him and come to some agreement for Christopher's sake.

His eyes were on the road now, so she couldn't judge his response, but his voice was entirely neutral as he said, 'I'm all yours, Cadence. I'll look forward to it. What are your own arrangements, Christopher?'

'Sorry! I was falling asleep,' confessed Christopher. 'My arrangements? I'll fit in the hotels and guides tomorrow and probably accompany one of the city tours, and later on I'll have to visit Kashmir and Delhi, but we mean to spend most of our time with you and Jaydev in Rajasthan. The guides and hotels there and at Agra I can inspect at my leisure.'

'I think you'll be satisfied with them,' commented Jon. 'As you know, I've kept in touch with the Rajasthan crowd. Sashi Kapur is still going strong with his inimitable store of anecdotes and jokes, and the latest Iverson recruit is the success story of the season. The tourists adore her—Sunila de Souza.'

Jahanara's hastily concealed smile told Cadence that Sunila de Souza was probably the woman in Jon

Steele's life, but her hopes of learning more were disappointed when the men went on to discuss more prosaic aspects of the Iverson Travel business. But— Sunila de Souza. It was an intriguing name, a mixture of Asian and Latin. There had to be a woman somewhere. She couldn't visualise Jon as a celibate.

Their hotel overlooked the harbour, an immense building of imperial splendour to which a new wing, almost as impressive as the old, had been added, and it was still early enough for the vast lobby to be virtually empty, so they were able to check in without any delay.

Cadence turned to Jon while Christopher was still busy at the counter. 'I'm going to shower, change and have breakfast again, but after that, I shall place myself in your hands.'

A glint appeared in the intensely blue eyes. 'The prospect is riveting. I can hardly wait!'

'What have I said?' Theatrically, she clapped a hand over her mouth, and then began to smile. 'Was it a very Freudian slip, Jon?'

Perhaps, she thought optimistically, if she could convince herself that the whole thing was more a cause for amusement than anything else, it would weigh less heavily on her and she would get over it the sooner. The danger lay in taking herself and her feelings too seriously.

Jon's look was inscrutable. 'Well, was it, darling? You tell me.'

She gave him her wide, friendly smile and looked significantly in Christopher's direction, shaking her head. 'That would really complicate things, wouldn't it? Let me tell you something about myself, Jon. I talk a lot of rubbish and I'm not on any account to be taken seriously.'

His mouth, which was beautiful, was touched by a

fleeting smile. 'Oh? Then precisely how shall I take you?'

'Just don't. Pretend I don't exist,' she advised airily, wondering if she had gone mad, standing here and flirting with her fiancé's best friend; she supposed it was flirtation of a sort and she was probably giving him altogether the wrong impression.

His suddenly sardonic gaze encompassed the suntanned length of her legs, the slimness of her hips below a narrow waist, firm young breasts and the purity and gracefully taut curve of the slender neck that bore her bright head, the unmarked face arresting in its youthful vitality and framed by sleek, burnished brown hair that the sun had streaked with honey-gold.

'That might just present a little difficulty,' he murmured drily, but his smile grew more relaxed and natural as Jahanara joined them. 'Where did you disappear to?'

'I thought Christopher and Cadence might be wanting breakfast, so I went to check the coffee shop's hours. They're open now, Cadence . . . Christopher.'

Christopher had joined them too now. 'I think I'll make it lunch, thanks, Jahanara. Jon, have you and Cadence made your arrangements? Then I'll see you whenever Cadence has exhausted either Bombay or you. I suppose even her energy has a limit, but it's never been discovered yet.'

'Christopher, you make the girl sound utterly terrifying!'

'I refuse to believe that you're intimidated!'

'I'm shaking in my shoes!' He threw Cadence a taunting smile. 'Incidentally, have you acquainted Cadence with the various rules regarding food and drink?'

'Don't drink the water, do you mean?' Cadence questioned.

'Yes, please be very careful, Cadence,' Jahanara adjured seriously. 'Especially here in Bombay. Even the local people are supposed to boil the water, though many take the risk, but we know how sick it makes European people.'

'And don't dismiss even the slightest sign of being unwell, but tell us,' added Jon.

'And Jon will dose you with his favourite remedy for all ailments—neat Scotch,' Christopher told her.

Jon laughed. 'It's often actually the only cure for some of the ills that afflict delicate Western stomachs.'

'Well, it's a good story, anyway,' Christopher retorted. 'Shall we go up, Cadence? They'll have our luggage up in a few minutes, they said. Be seeing you, you two.'

Cadence was relieved to find that Christopher wasn't disposed to question her about her opinion of Jon at this early juncture, especially as she was unsure of exactly what she felt.

They parted at the door of her room which was next to his, and with her excitement at actually being in India undiminished, Cadence went straight to the long window, opening it and stepping out on to the tiny balcony, to gaze enthralled at the scene below and the vast bay beyond. The soft morning light was brightening as the day grew older, the colourful crowds beginning to appear, going about their business, the sound of their voices and the city traffic rising evocatively to her ears, while dominating the entire scene was a mighty edifice on a concrete apron. Cadence didn't need to be told it was the Gateway of India, and she stood awhile watching the distant figures of men, women and children as they slipped into the cool dark shadows cast by the vast imperial arch, reminder of an unforgettable era.

She was recalled by a knock at the door signalling

the arrival of her luggage, and as soon as she was alone again she got busy, eager to be out and experiencing all that Bombay had to offer and aware, too, that she and Jon Steele needed to have a talk, the sort of candid discussion that would smooth away whatever it was that lay between them and ensure that their future relationship was as harmonious as Christopher would wish for the two most important people in his life.

She showered and dressed in a loose cool top of soft Egyptian cotton in the vivid saffron that suited her so well, belting it over white cotton jeans so that the slenderness of her waist and her height were attractively emphasised, and finally donning comfortable sandals.

Downstairs once more, she cashed a traveller's cheque with the cashier and went into the coffee shop to order the breakfast she had been looking forward to, beginning with mango juice and finishing with two leisurely cups of coffee, enjoying watching the international crowd about her, Indians, Europeans and other Asians of both sexes, but men only from the Middle East.

She was halfway through the second cup of coffee when Jon Steele appeared beside her table.

'May I?' He didn't wait for her permission but sat down opposite her, ordering coffee for himself from the waiter who appeared instantly—he had that sort of commanding presence, Cadence reflected, surveying him ironically.

'I thought I'd find you here,' said Jon. 'I didn't want to ring through to your room in case I woke Christopher. I imagine he's out for the count by now?'

'I expect so. I wouldn't know. We've got separate rooms,' Cadence told him pleasantly.

His dark eyebrows rose slightly, but he smiled too. 'Very discreet! Then you won't be too disappointed when our hosts in Rajasthan separate you. Jaydev has never obeyed a rule, social or religious, if it didn't suit him, but appearances are a different matter—and not out of any sort of hypocrisy, but simply because he's affectionate enough to indulge his wife, who is somewhat more conventional than he.'

'Was his father really a maharaja?'

'Yes, the last maharaja of their principality and as unorthodox as Jaydev. For instance, he was one of those who campaigned for the Untouchables. Jaydev himself is a Colonel and he and his family still occupy part of the palace, as Christopher will have told you. His father was one of those shrewder princes who went into business, politics and so on, so when the privy purses were finally done away with in the Seventies, the family were well prepared and not reduced to selling family heirlooms.'

'And we're actually going to stay in the private apartments of the palace! Oh, it's all so exciting. And today—Bombay! I can hardly wait!' Cadence smiled at him. 'But I'll let you have your coffee first.'

'You'll let me? How very generous of you, Cadence,' Jon commented sarcastically.

She went on smiling. 'I told you, you mustn't take me seriously. I just talk like that sometimes, you know. Anyway, we ought to have a talk, don't you think?'

'A talk? A specific talk? No, I can't say the necessity has occurred to me,' he taunted amusedly. 'What did you want to talk about?'

The waiter arrived with his coffee at that moment, and Cadence found herself staring at Jon with mounting resentment. She had meant to be frank and friendly, but to hell with it! He made it impossible. Just by sitting there, by living, breathing, existing, he made it impossible! She had only to look at him—she had only to experience the scorching intensity of his vivid gaze and reel under the dynamic impact of his vitality—to feel this angry confusion welling up inside her.

'Oh well, perhaps I was wrong, perhaps it's nothing talking can straighten out,' she allowed sharply when the waiter had gone. 'Perhaps you've just got a naturally nasty disposition and can't help yourself!'

He shook his head in mock regret. 'And there I was, thinking I was doing quite well at showing you how nice I can be.'

'And why should you want to do that?' Cadence pounced.

'For Christopher's sake, why else?' he retorted indifferently. 'The man wants us to get on.'

His answer should have pleased her, but instead she found her annoyance growing, to a point where she could scarcely sit still in her chair.

'Tell me, Jon!' Her eyes flashed imperatively. 'When you and Christopher were boys, did you swear one of those blood oaths? You know, cut yourselves with penknives or something, mix your blood and swear eternal brotherhood?'

'My God!' He was laughing helplessly. 'Where did you get such an idea?'

'Oh, I think I saw it in a movie,' she answered vaguely. 'Did you?'

'No!' He was still laughing, but suddenly he stopped. 'I get it! You're jealous. I thought there was something.'

'As a matter of fact, I was about to ask if you were jealous of me,' she told him coldly.

Jon's eyes narrowed. 'Cadence, just what sort of relationship do you imagine Christopher and I have?'

'Oh, nothing like that,' she assured him dismissively. 'But you see, Christopher told me about how when he was a teenager and too shy to ask girls out, you used to do it for him, and you even chose the girls.'

He looked amused. 'He told you about that, did he?'

'Christopher tells me everything!'

'Cadence, sweetheart, no man tells a woman everything,' he contradicted her cynically.

'Christopher does. Anyway, you didn't choose me for him, did you? He picked me all by himself.' She was challenging him and her pride at having won Christopher's interest and love rang a clear, true note in her attractive voice.

'Oh, undoubtedly, he saw you first,' drawled Jon. 'A pity. I'd have enjoyed . . . taking you seriously. Or otherwise.'

She suppressed a traitorous smile. 'Is that any way to talk to your best friend's fiancée? You don't like me, do you?'

'How can I say? I've only just met you.'

'Well, there's something! You said so yourself.'

'Cadence,' he sighed, looking both entertained and exasperated, 'let's not get too honest—for Christopher's sake. It's harder to forget the truth than it is a lie.'

'Yes, well, that's really what I wanted to talk to you about,' she explained. 'For Christopher's sake, can't we try to get on? At least give the appearance of doing so?'

'And behave like civilised, rational adults?' he mocked. 'Yes, we can try. I think we should.'

Briefly she wondered if they were talking about the same thing. If Jon refused to name the truth, how was she to know if he referred to hostility or lust? For Cadence, who had never in her life dissembled about her feelings, it was especially frustrating, and she moved irritably. Of course, if was possible that the physical attraction was on her side alone, since he had given no real evidence of feeling anything similar, unless she counted the sexual connotation contained in certain of his remarks, but he probably talked that way to all women. There were men like that, she knew, those who were unable to conceive of any male-female interaction being entirely free of sex, men who regarded both themselves and women as being purely sex objects, at least in relation to each other.

'I do want Christopher to be happy, you see,' she said softly, just so that he wasn't in any doubt.

Jon seemed about to make some quick retort, changed his mind and gave her a long, coolly contemplative look. Finally one corner of his mouth quirked in a way she found utterly fascinating, not quite a smile but very attractive—endearing, almost.

'You really do love him, don't you?'

'Yes.' She had thought it was obvious, since she never troubled to hide it.

'Yes.' Another of those long looks, but his expression was so enigmatic that she couldn't guess what he might be thinking. Then he picked up his cup of coffee and drained it in one long draught, causing Cadence to wince as it must still have been extremely hot. 'Well, if you've finished, let's get moving and introduce you to Bombay.'

Walking beside him through the lobby a few minutes later, Cadence wasn't sure if they had settled anything. They had talked, it was true, even if they had not done so with complete candour, but had anything really been resolved?

'Isn't Jahanara coming with us?'

'No. She has a duty visit to an elderly aunt living here and decided to make it this morning.' Jon paused. 'Are you placing yourself in my hands, sweetheart, or do you have some preferences?'

'Well, yes, I do,' she admitted smilingly.

'I thought so. You're not exactly a passive little woman, are you?'

'I can't help it.' She was unapologetic.

'Well, let's hear it?'

'The truth is I'm a Philistine, Jon.' She was discovering that she liked making him smile. It made him so very attractive. 'Culture has its place——'

'In museums!'

'Yes, and while I'd love to fit in some if there's time, first of all I want to hit the streets, see the people.'

'As long as you're not planning on turning it into a shopping expedition! All right, we'll go on foot to start with and pick up a taxi when you've had enough or want to do something different.'

Outside, Cadence was instantly fascinated by the crowds, the noise and colour; the exotic garments— turbans, dhotis, saris, punjabis; and the jewellery, the anklets and bangles often adorning even girls not past the toddling stage, finger- and toe-rings, earrings and nose-studs; and she was amused by the persistence of the hawkers who followed them about, sometimes for the length of several blocks.

'But I must just buy a pair of those sandals, Jon. It will be my only purchase, I promise you!' Cadence's face was alight with enthusiasm.

'All right!' His exasperation was touched with indulgence. 'But don't pay the price he's asking unless you want to earn his contempt.'

'I can't get over the number of cinemas!' she exclaimed a few minutes later, the transaction completed and the flat sandals stowed in her spacious shoulder bag.

'India produces more films in a year than Hollywood—mostly highly sentimental epics.' He paused. 'Tell me about yourself, Cadence Reay.'

'There's not much to tell,' she laughed. 'I grew up in a nice suburb in London, I enjoyed school and I loved my parents and my brothers, Murray and Neil, and still do. I've worked for Iverson Travel for over four years, and six months ago I met Christopher. That's all really.'

'And that's it? Nothing complicated, no hidden hang-ups, no vices?'

'I am . . . as I am.' Cadence laughed a little wryly because it seemed so silly, stating the obvious.

'And even your future in-laws approve of you,' added Jon with just the slightest note of mockery, but nothing unkind. 'Both Aubrey and Stephanie have written to me, full of enthusiasm about this engagement.'

'I adore them, don't you?'

'I owe them a lot.' He was suddenly oddly expressionless.

'They adore you,' she pointed out, dissatisfied with his answer.

'Yes. I know.' Abruptly, he changed the subject. 'What else do you want to do this morning?'

Cadence turned her bright smooth head, her honey eyes thoughtful as she looked at him. She would have loved to probe further, to persist until this newest riddle was answered, but she sensed that he was not a man who could be coaxed or goaded or worn down, if he didn't want to be. His will, like his vitality, was even stronger than her own. Perhaps that was why she felt threatened by him for so much of the time . . .

Realising it was pointless, she dropped her voice sepulchrally. 'The Towers of Silence, Jon? And the vultures!'

He laughed, relaxing. 'Not quite so uncomplicated after all. Have you always been such a ghoul? We'll find a taxi.'

Cadence would never forget her first day in India, that land where the passions of its many peoples had written a turbulent history, both remote and recent, and made the future a continuation of the adventure, for the paradoxes of conflict and unity, triumph and tragedy, humour and pathos would be part of India still and responsible for the fascination she had exerted for so long.

The Towers of Silence and the waiting vultures were alien enough to satisfy even Cadence's taste for the novel, and she shuddered even while she appreciated the simple logic that lay behind the Parsee manner of dealing with death.

Jon also showed her the so-called hanging gardens, financed by that wealthy community, descendants of Persia's Zoroastrian fireworshippers, constructed over a reservoir to prevent the vultures polluting the city's water by dropping pieces of flesh as they flew over; but there were homely things too, that made Bombay endearing as well as awesome, ordinary things and yet essentially part of the Indian experience—strolling among the crowds of local people in Kalama Nehru Park, Indian music coming tinnily from loudspeakers in the trees; sipping cold drinks in an open-air café; pavement vendors mixing strange concoctions and wrapping them in leaves for sale to the local people; an unfortunate dog being persuaded to perform simple tricks between busy lanes of traffic; and, everywhere, cricket games or practice sessions in progress, on large well-tended fields or on tiny rough allotments between old grey buildings, a fierce national passion preponderant even over that for the cinema.

Like any other city, Bombay combined both beauty and ugliness. Beauty was in the marine drive round the bay and in Hindu and Jain temples. The greatest ugliness, as far as Cadence was concerned, was the sight of poor prostitutes kept in cages, and she suspected that Jon had been testing her in some way by telling their driver to bring them to this district, quoting her wish to see 'the people', but she refused to pretend to emotions other than those she felt—mostly pity in this case—and Jon made no comment about her reaction, merely telling their driver that they had seen enough here.

In contrast, their next stop was at the house where Gandhi had stayed when visiting Bombay, now the repository of books and letters pertaining to his famous life, and Cadence spent an absorbed half hour wandering about an upstairs room where the main events of the Mahatma's life were depicted by the most incredibly realistic little dolls, the painstaking work of one devoted woman.

Down in the street once more, Jon turned to her.

'And now, Cadence, we're returning to the hotel. Anything else can wait until tomorrow or the next morning—we don't leave for Rajasthan until the afternoon. You may not be tired, but you're probably slightly dehydrated. Air travel alone does that, and then the heat here is more intense than anything you've been used to.'

'I've noticed how you've been plying me with soft drinks all around town,' she commented. She had been grateful for them too, although she hadn't thought to wonder what was causing her excessive need for liquid.

'Somehow I don't think Christopher would be exactly thrilled if I returned you to him in a state of collapse,' Jon said drily.

'Back to the hotel it is, then. You see, I can be a passive little woman after all!'

'When it suits you, yes. I'm under no illusions, Cadence.'

'I'm truly grateful to you for showing me around and taking such good care of me,' she told him a few minutes later as, horn blaring almost constantly, their taxi swept, dodged and ploughed its way through the city traffic. 'I've adored it all, and I just hope you haven't been too bored.'

'No. I expected to be, but there's something about youthful enthusiasm that's highly rewarding.'

Cadence wasn't sure if he was making fun of her, so she simply gave him a brilliant smile before turning to gaze through the window at the colourful masses she would never cease to find fascinating. The truth was that while she had enjoyed herself immensely, she had not always been fully at ease in Jon's company, and whenever he had touched her, as he had occasionally, placing a guiding hand on her bare arm as they moved through a crowd, she had been acutely aware of the fact that physically he stirred her as no other man had.

It seemed to her that each of them acted a part, denying certain truths, and while that was exactly what she had proposed in the coffee shop that morning, it was not something that came either naturally or easily to Cadence.

But desire was transitory, she comforted herself; she would get over it because it wouldn't last, and so there was no point in admitting the truth to either Jon or Christopher and thereby causing unnecessary tension. Christopher was the man she loved, the man she was going to marry . . .

By the time she had rested and spent time alone with Christopher, Cadence's philosophy was firmer, more fixed. Just seeing him had reassured her—it was he whom she loved—and so, when they dined at the Tanjore that night, with Jon Steele and Jahanara Khan, she was completely happy and at ease once more.

Her mobile face alight with enjoyment, whether she was watching the little dancing girl with the flirtatious eyes and the squatting musicians playing their exotic instruments, or sharing with Christopher all she had seen that day, Cadence was still vibrantly aware of an enigmatic blue gaze whenever it came to rest on her, but now she refused to wonder what thoughts lay behind it.

And, watching her, observing her vivacity and the pleasure Christopher Iverson took in it, Jon Steele reflected that she reminded him of nothing so much as a young lioness, revelling in her strength and youth, innocently playful and all unaware of her own deadly power.

It was a power that could so easily prove fatal, to either Christopher or himself—or to both of them.

CHAPTER THREE

COLONEL JAYDEV NAYAR's splendid air-conditioned cars raced through the darkness of the Rajasthan desert, sprucely liveried drivers at the wheel of each, Christopher and Cadence in the back of one, Jon and Jahanara in the other.

This was luxury, Cadence reflected peacefully, and it was especially so after that bumpy, crowded flight up from Bombay, although her boundless curiosity about other human beings and her sheer zest for every experience life offered had made the trip intriguing. There had been that Sikh across the aisle, who had looked so unapproachable and then proved so amenable to answering her questions about his people, and then there had been the noisily boisterous cricket team which had boarded at Ahmadabad, still jubilant over some victory ... She was learning that India was a country of extreme contrasts and intense enthusiasms that often amounted to passions and sometimes to fanaticism.

And here was another contrast.

'Jaydev certainly does things in style,' she sighed happily. 'You've known him quite a long time, haven't you?'

'Yes. Jon first met him when he started paying visits to India as a young man, and then I got to know him when I first made the trip,' Christopher explained. 'I suppose he's one of our closest mutual friends, although he's some years older than us, about forty, I think. He's stayed with us at home, we've played polo together ... That's one of his major passions, incidentally, and cricket is another, but he works as hard as he plays. His father, the last maharaja, was wise long before many others, realising that the princely states would eventually have to accede when India gained her Independence; he made investments with that in mind, and Jaydev and his brothers and cousins have followed that tradition and are all wealthy men.'

'I know it was inevitable and for the best, but there's a sad side,' Cadence confided. 'So much romance was lost with the end of the maharajas, nawabs and the rest.'

'I don't think it has truly vanished from this state yet; there are reminders of the various royal families all over the place; and don't you think the Indian government was paying a compliment to the romantic tradition of the Rajputs when they named this area Rajasthan? You're glad to be here, aren't you?'

'Ecstatic!'

'And you enjoyed Bombay?' He was solicitous.

'Of course! Especially when you were free to share it with me.'

But the demands of his position with Iverson Travel hadn't taken up that much of his time and she had passed some of it entertainingly enough, slipping beneath the vast span of the Gateway of India with Jon and Jahanara to board a small boat, packed with local trippers, for an exhilarating trip round the bay. Yesterday afternoon had been devoted to shopping and more shopping with Christopher, and Cadence was now equipped with several of the outfits currently fashionable in India, including a sari and a punjabi, plus an exquisitely carved, broad, thick ivory bangle with a silver clasp which Christopher had bought for her. This morning, with Cadence suddenly stricken with guilt about her own Philistinism, they had made a hasty visit to the Prince of Wales museum, and this afternoon they had checked out of their hotel and caught the Air India flight which had brought them to Rajasthan.

'How are you and Jon getting on?' Christopher asked now.

She had known he would issue the question at some stage, but she still had no real answer. Silently, she reviewed the last two days, and realised that she had not been alone with Jon again since that initial exploration of Bombay. Had it merely happened that way by chance, or was it something he had deliberately engineered?

On a superficial level, she had believed they were getting on tolerably well, and so they should be—she had worked at it! Knowing how much it meant to Christopher, she had been careful not to challenge or antagonise Jon in any way, taking pains to be friendly and uncontroversial, and to a degree she had been successful. There had been no clashes between them, nothing to distress Christopher ... On the surface, their relationship was a polite, neutral sort of friendship, not close but entirely harmonious.

On the surface. At a deeper level, she had continued to be aware of a hostility and a tension which, on her side at least, had much to do with the way Jon affected her physically. Cadence understood her own body and its urges; she knew she was at present attracted to Jon, but she remained confident that sooner or later the fever would fade. Sooner, she hoped, because it wasn't a comfortable thing and she wanted to be able to give her undivided love and desire to Christopher. So far, as it was, she had only been able to feel relief that Christopher had wanted no more than to make a little very light love to her since their arrival in India, as she knew she would not have been able to respond unreservedly while her flesh was distracted by Jon Steele, however completely her heart and mind belonged to Christopher.

That in itself was enough to make her resent Jon, but her irritable frustration was increased by the fact that she simply did not know what his feelings were. He seemed to have placed himself at a distance where she was concerned, and if he had done so deliberately, the reason could be any one of a number of possibilities.

'Cadence?' Christopher prompted when she had been silent for some time.

'Sorry! I was thinking. The truth is, I don't know, Christo. I suppose I'm still getting to know Jon. He's . . . rather an enigma, isn't he?' she ventured.

'Do you think so?' Christopher sounded faintly surprised. 'Yes, well, I realise he might strike you that way. I've known him for most of my life, and I suppose I understand him.'

'Why is he unmarried?'

He laughed. 'First of all, Jon doesn't love easily, and then he enjoys playing the field—as most men do until they're lucky enough to find someone like you.'

'I'm the lucky one, darling.' She touched his hand. 'And is that what Jon's doing now? Playing the field?'

'I asked him about that,' he admitted. 'I gather he's had something going with this Sunila de Souza, one of Iverson Travel's new guides in Rajasthan, a Goan girl. But he tells me he's trying to ease out of it now.'

'I wonder how Sunila feels about it.'

Perhaps a hint of censure betrayed her, although she hadn't meant to sound tart. Christopher's hand closed gently round hers.

'Cadence, perhaps I should have told you so that you'd understand. You . . . No, we have to accept that

Jon is not a kind man, save to those few people he genuinely cares about.'

'I didn't mean to sound critical,' she apologised. 'I expect there's a reason, isn't there? I mean, what's made him so hard? The start he had in life, losing his parents so young and so tragically, the way your mother told me?'

'Oh, he won't have that sort of excuse made for him at any price,' Christopher told her reluctantly. 'He insists that it's just the way he is naturally. He won't concede to having been shaped by any experience.'

'Steele by nature as well as by name,' Cadence commented lightly.

'Perhaps.' Christopher didn't sound entirely convinced. 'Oh, you'll understand when you know him better.'

'I hope you're not disappointed in me for not understanding already.'

'Darling, the last three days have been pretty crowded, and anyway, I've got a twenty-five-year start on you where Jon's concerned,' laughed Christopher, releasing her hand and lifting his arm to put it about her, lightly encircling her shoulders. 'Life at the palace will be more leisurely, the three of us will be able to spend more time together. Here's the town coming up, those lights ahead. The palace is out a little way into the desert on the other side. The other car will be stopping to drop Jahanara off at her home in town. She travels out to the palace on those mornongs when Jon requires her services, she tells me.'

'She thinks you're very romantic,' Cadence told him teasingly.

Christopher laughed with slight embarrassment. 'It seems to be her favourite word. I suppose the two of you sit around discussing Jon and me when you're alone?'

Cadence dropped her head to his shoulder. 'And don't you and Jon do exactly the same thing?'

'Well, and why not? Only——' Christopher halted thoughtfully. 'You know, it's just struck me? Jon rarely mentions you, never questions me about you. I wonder why that is?'

Cadence raised her head. She hated to distress him, but she had to warn him, armour him against possible disappointment.

'Did it ever occur to you that he might take a dislike to me, darling?' she asked gently.

'Everyone likes you, Cady, you know that.' Christopher refused to take her suggestion seriously.

'Flattery will get you everywhere!' she retorted. 'No, seriously, Christo, you and your parents have always told me what an exceptional man Jon Steele is, and perhaps he's the exception in this instance too.'

'Someone who doesn't like you!'

'Imagine it!'

'I can't,' he laughed. 'No, he's probably reserving judgement, my love. He does care about me and my family, you know, and he probably wants to be sure we'll be happy together ... Though God knows, I've told him often enough how much you mean to me.'

'Tell me too,' she invited him mischievously, needing reassurance for some reason, an unusual requirement for her, but the conversation had done nothing to ease her confusion and uncertainty.

'Don't I tell you all the time?'

Nevertheless, he told her again, in so many ways, and so entrancingly that Cadence was too absorbed to take much notice of the town through which they passed, a small city really, save that most of the buildings were very old and that the oldest part of all was actually a walled city within a city.

The palace itself, a few kilometres out in the rough, steep-hilled desert terrain, was a honey-coloured poem, a dream, a fairytale, set in vast grounds. Floodlit from outside, it was all filigreed stone, ornate, massive and beautiful, a tribute to the infinity of man's imagination.

The interior was equally breathtaking, marble-inlaid and mirror-studded, the vast chambers a spectacular reminder of days when the Indian princes possessed wealth beyond dreams and courts numbering hundreds or even thousands, able to indulge their every proclivity, with jewels of fabulous fame, wives and concubines of legendary beauty, all the hawks they desired, tiger hunts and sports events involving complicated planning so that they were simply a continuation of the luxury of palace life.

In these more prosaic times, however, the eldest son of the last maharaja and his family occupied but one wing of the palace, though even that was stupendous in its spread and labyrinthine ways, while the rest of the palace, like so many all over what was once Rajputana, had been turned into a luxury hotel with certain rooms maintained as they had been in those glorious days of decadence and chivalry, but museums now, unlived in.

There were plenty of servants too, as Cadence was to learn, but, democratically, it was Colonel Nayar and his wife themselves who admitted them, and later, after they had all had a drink and just as Jon was arriving, having delivered Jahanara to her home and lingered to reassure her brother that no harm had befallen her in Bombay, it was Padmini Nayar who showed Cadence to her room—though chamber would be a more appropriate word, she thought when she saw it.

'These were once the quarters of a favourite concubine,' she was told by the graceful, quiet-voiced

Padmini whose sari was deliberately simple enough to emphasise the flashing magnificence of her jewels.

'It looks good enough for a wife,' Cadence laughed, surveying the sumptuous suite, translucent marble floor strewn with the loveliest silk rugs she had ever seen, their colours subtle, yet vibrant and glowing too.

'Oh, my darling, the concubines were often far more favoured than the wives,' Padmini told her. 'Some of them were spoilt little madams by all accounts. The maharaja later married this particular girl when one of his wives died, whereupon the number one wife had her poisoned, so in honouring her, he killed her.'

'Poor man! He must have been devastated—and furious! What happened to the wife?'

'Nothing. She happened to be the mother of the maharaja's favourite son, and the other girl probably was no real threat to her, but there was always intrigue in those days, and a lot of it originated in the women's quarters. Insecurity and boredom were the causes, I think. The wife continued to be honoured for her son's sake and was given her own palace, and when the maharaja died, as chief queen she had the honour of sharing his pyre.' Padmini's pretty smile flashed out. 'These are better days. Now, do you have everything you require, Cadence? I see your luggage is here. If there's anything you need, just pick up the telephone . . . Dinner is late tonight as I thought you would want to refresh yourself after the flight and the drive, and Jaydev and Christopher will have a lot to talk about. Come down in about an hour's time. You won't get lost?'

Left alone, Cadence let her eyes travel round the huge room once more, her mind filled with questions about the luckless creature who had once occupied these quarters. Had the poor girl married her maharaja in love or fear, or in triumph, heedless of the consequences? Had anyone recorded her thoughts and feelings, or only the bare facts of the story?

She shivered. Padmini was right: these were better days. Fear must have been one of the most prevalent emotions in the princely courts of those times. She would have hated to have been one of the women, her status, her life, dependent on her ability to please her lord or bear sons, and then if she survived all life's cruel chances, to end on a blazing pyre, along with her surviving rivals.

Her bathroom was as luxurious as her bedroom, and Cadence revelled in its marble splendour for longer than she had intended. She had just finished drying herself and donning fresh underwear when there was a knock at the door. Quickly she pulled on her thin cotton robe, tying the belt about her waist as she went to open the door.

'What the hell have you been saying to Christopher?' Jon Steele's eyes were blazing, bluer than ever.

'What? Jon?' Shocked, Cadence stared at him. 'Jon! What are you doing?'

He had pushed past her into the room and was closing the door.

'Why did you do it, Cadence?' he asked with bitter anger. 'Why have you made trouble? I really thought you loved Christopher.'

'Well, of course I do,' she snapped. 'What are you talking about? What am I supposed to have done?'

He drew a breath and spoke slowly and clearly: 'I have just had Christopher telling me that you don't find my attitude towards you quite—normal. That you suspect me of disliking you or something.'

'Well, what's wrong with that?' retorted Cadence, growing angrier by the second. 'He asked me, and I told him.'

'And thereby undid all the work I've put in over the

last couple of days,' Jon accused tautly, his dark face hard with fury. 'My God, I've really gone out of my way not to disturb his peace of mind, and then with a few words you——'

'Well, why should you have to act a part, Jon?' she cut in defensively. 'And why should Christopher be deceived? I wanted to warn him, prepare him for the truth——'

'The truth!' His laugh was harsh, empty of amusement. 'And how do you think he's going to like the truth, once it hits him, as it will now that you've got him wondering about my reaction to you?'

'I know he expects everyone to like me, but that's because he loves me——'

'Like you! And since he—presumably—also desires you, doesn't he also expect other men to do so?' taunted Jon.

Cadence stared at him, her parted lips quivering slightly as she understood him.

'Oh, damn,' she said quietly. This would make it all so much harder.

His mouth curved in self-mockery. 'Christopher and I have always had the same taste in women, and do you know why? Because I shaped his taste. And yet you're nothing like the other women who've passed through our lives ... You, Cadence! You're not even truly beautiful, but you're young and alive and I want you. I want all that youth and life and colour, I want to possess them——'

'Jon ...'

For once in her life, Cadence was bereft of speech. His words were performing a sort of magic and she was shaken by a surge of emotion she couldn't identify, robbed of her anger.

'I've watched you these last days and I've wanted you, so much that it's a constant ache, and it's been that way since I first saw you in Bombay. I saw you among the crowds at that airport and I knew at once that you had to be Christopher's fiancée and that I wanted you, God help me. I don't dislike you, Cadence, but my God, I resent you, for what you've done to me—for what you'll still do to Christopher and me!'

'Jon, I have to——'

'I'm actually obsessed with you!' He was still angry, and disgusted. 'I want to touch you and hold you and have you; I want you when all that terrible strength of yours is gone and you're weak with wanting; I want you when all your talk and laughter are stopped and silenced and you can't speak for desire. I look at you now, and I want you, and I can't help myself——'

Cadence had hardly noticed the step he took towards her, but now she was in his arms, his mouth swooping to devour hers, and there was nothing in the world she could do to stop what was happening.

There were no teasing preliminaries. Their kiss was instantly deeply intimate, shockingly erotic, and she felt as if her blood caught fire, desire a leaping, frantic force she had never known before, intensified as much by the knowledge that Jon wanted her as by the fact that, finally, he was holding her in the way her flesh had craved ever since she had first seen him.

The kiss went on and on, yet it ended too soon, and her soft moan invited another, and the hot melting sensation that began in the centre of her femininity spread through all her being, making her pliant, yielding, as she clung to him.

They had been standing near the door and Cadence was hardly aware of the journey they made across the palatial room to the low, wide, silk-covered bed, hands and mouths frenziedly discovering each other.

Jon had loosened the belt of her robe and she

shrugged out of it completely before collapsing on the bed and pulling him down to her, fingers tearing at his shirt buttons as she was consumed with the need to know his flesh on hers.

She was gasping, mindless with hunger as his mouth claimed hers again in a long, bruising kiss, and her hands moved all about his burning flesh, trembling fingers discovering the hardness of his muscles beneath the taut skin. She writhed against him, whimpering softly in the back of her throat, unable to be still, utterly dominated by the sensations he was inducing, everything else in the world and beyond forgotten. Damnation could follow and she would not care.

'Stop me, Cadence, you've got to stop me,' Jon was instructing harshly even as he was removing her flimsy white bra.

'I can't,' she groaned, opening her eyes. 'That's what I was trying to tell you, I've felt it too . . . ever since Bombay. I want you, Jon!'

'Oh, God.'

Passion-glazed blue dropped to her swollen breasts, the nipples hard and hot, aching for his touch.

'Touch me,' she whispered hoarsely, straining upward towards him, and a shivering little cry of delight escaped her as he complied compulsively, one hand closing over a breast, and she felt the thrusting peak throb against his hard palm.

It wasn't enough, though, and her incoherent pleas were answered when he bent his head to her breasts. His mouth was warm and moist, the most voluptuous thing she had ever known, his tongue circling first one nipple and then the other, and rasping over them again and again. Cadence's slender fingers tightened convulsively in his dark hair, relaxed and slid down to dig into his powerful shoulders, and she moaned softly with pleasure and satisfaction as he took the impossibly taut flesh gently between his teeth, threatening an exquisite pain.

The sexual excitement between them was so intense, a live, quivering thing that made their bodies vibrate with their need, and to Cadence it seemed so right, so natural, that she was actually happy, deliriously so, with no thought for anything beyond the tangle of their limbs and flesh on flesh. The world contained her and Jon, and they contained the world. There was nothing else and no one else.

Jon's dark head was raised once more, then his harsh mouth lowered to her flushed one again. Cadence's eyes closed, but she still saw his dark, drawn face, tight with the driving intensity of his passion, intent blue eyes burning, burning ... His hands were at her breasts again, at her sides, on her and beneath her, lifting her, pressing her down against the bed again, sliding over her waist and hips, crossing her flat stomach, caressing her long slim thighs, stroking upward again.

He shifted, moving over her and on to her, his mouth still sensually invading hers, and she stirred restlessly beneath him, straining to be even closer, to achieve the ultimate closeness, the final rapture.

It was miraculous, the thought came to her as her aching breasts were crushed against the hardness of his chest, the cloud of dark hair covering his firm flesh softly rasping her agonisingly sensitised nipples, an exquisite torture. It was miraculous that they could be together like this, she and Jon, convulsed with desire for each other, so perfectly matched, when she——

When she loved Christopher, she recalled.

Jon's swollen arousal promised unknown fulfilment, but suddenly her shame was greater than the temptation to snatch at ecstasy. She slid her mouth aside from his.

'Jon, I think we have to stop . . . now,' she panted against his hard cheek. 'I'm in love with Christopher and I can't . . . I can't be unfaithful to him!'

He looked down into her flushed, unhappy face, and Cadence felt her heart contract with anguish, seeing the agony it cost him to accept her words and bring himself under control. Her hands were at his shoulders as he lifted himself away from her, and almost she drew him back, wanting to ease his pain and let him take the pleasure he sought.

'Yes. Christopher,' he remembered flatly.

Cadence lifted a hand, laying it against his cheek, wanting to comfort him while she herself needed comfort.

'I'm sorry,' she offered futilely.

He moved away to stand up, buttoning his shirt. 'You'd be sorrier still, and so would I, if we'd . . . if we hadn't stopped. Oh, God, Cadence!' he added violently. 'Why did you have to want me as well? It only makes it worse.'

'I know.' She sat up and put on her bra although she knew she would have to shower. Her skin was glistening with perspiration, his and hers mingled, and her body was still vibrant with longing, so sensitive that she knew if he touched her again she would not be able to stop him a second time.

Jon picked up her robe and tossed it to her, then stood watching her, his eyes suddenly warily alert.

'Are you going to tell Christopher?' he asked abruptly.

'I don't know,' Cadence responded uncertainly, her tone utterly sad. 'It depends . . . This won't last, will it? I won't always feel this way, not . . . not when——'

'Not when you love Christopher,' he supplied harshly. 'And you do, don't you? So let's get this straight! Your reasoning is that since you're unlikely to go on wanting me and since nothing actually happened——'

'A hell of a lot happened!' she flared furiously, and he acknowledged it with a taut smile.

'But not the ultimate betrayal. So, in the light of that, you see no need to confess the deed to Christopher . . . since the deed is incomplete. And you so honest, Cadence!' he taunted.

'I know, I know!' she agreed. 'Why are you so unsympathetic? You were involved just as much as me.'

'Agreed.'

'Oh, hell!' Cadence stood up, belting her robe. 'But where the truth causes pain, unnecessary pain I mean, is it such an admirable thing?'

'A clever quibble, darling,' Jon mocked.

'Do you want me to tell him?' she asked incredulously.

He was silent a moment before shrugging with a wry smile. 'No. You're right, of course, Cadence. I'm just being bloody-minded because I'm hurting from having failed to have my evil way with you!'

She couldn't help smiling at that, but she sobered instantly. 'I feel so bitterly ashamed,' she confided guiltily. 'And not telling Christopher will make it worse. I've never had to keep anything secret before, not from anyone!'

'You'll get over it,' Jon assured her callously. 'As I said earlier, you've got a terrible strength—an appalling resilience. You'll get over it and you'll marry Christopher and make him very happy and spend the rest of your life congratulating yourself on having forsaken the principle of honesty in favour of the

principle of keeping Christopher happy. Honesty is
the best policy versus ignorance is bliss!'

'I don't think that's funny,' she snapped. 'God, I
don't know how I can want someone I detest so much!
It's a mystery to me. And you, Jon? What will you be
doing while I'm congratulating myself? Christopher
expects you to be part of our lives. He even wants you
to be godfather to our first child.'

'And if I refuse, he'll wonder why. Oh, it will all
have blown over by then, sweetheart, and we'll be able
to laugh at ourselves. In the meantime . . .' He paused.
'It won't happen again, Cadence. I'll see you at
dinner.'

And there wasn't much time left before dinner, she
realised as the door closed behind him. She stared
round the lavishly appointed room, troubled eyes
finally coming to rest on the rumpled soft crimson silk
covering the low bed, and her stomach tightened at the
evidence of erotic intimacy.

After all, times hadn't changed at the palace. Sex
still lay at the root of resentful feelings and
disturbance, just as it had been responsible for much
of the evil and intrigue, the whispered plots, secret
schemes and mysterious deaths that abounded in the
days of the princes. Perhaps the erotic, dangerous
atmosphere of those days still lingered in these
apartments, influencing all those who entered them.

With a short angry laugh, Cadence strode into the
bathroom. Atmosphere be damned! She knew what it
was. If not some complex chemistry, then it was sheer,
unhappy chance that was responsible for this
attraction between herself and Jon Steele—and she
was furious with that chance, with the fate that had
never let her down before.

She was also furious with herself for having so
nearly betrayed Christopher, and most furious of all

with Jon, especially for his taunting attitude just now, although she knew it was frustration that had made him lash out like that.

Damn it, wasn't she frustrated herself? She still wanted him; not even guilt could change that.

'Not yet,' she muttered optimistically. But she would get over it. She would! She had to!

Dressed in a simple straight cream dress drawn in at the waist by a fine silken stretch belt with an exquisitely enamelled clasp, she left her room, losing herself a few times, but there was always a smartly uniformed servant about to set her right, so unfailingly that she began to suspect they deliberately stationed themselves at strategic points when visitors were newly in residence.

Finally she found the others sitting with drinks in the large drawing-room at one side of an even larger reception room.

'I'm so sorry. Have I kept you waiting?' Cadence was one of those people who commanded attention and they all looked at her as she entered, but it was Jon's enigmatic blue glance she was conscious of first, and only afterwards Christopher's loving smile, and her guilt increased.

Please God, it doesn't show, she thought fervently. He would be so hurt if he knew, and she couldn't bear that.

'No problem.' Jaydev had got to his feet. 'Jon has only just joined us too.'

'Showering, Jon?' Her voice was as sweet and cold as ice-cream as her honey eyes rested on his slightly damp hair.

'Of course. A cold one,' he claimed drily.

'Oh, no!' Padmini was shocked. 'Is there a problem with the hot water?'

Jaydev, a big well-built man, roared with laughter.

'It's a joke, my dear. I'll explain it to you later. Never mind, Jon, my friend! Sunila is due in at the end of the week. Cadence, what will you drink?'

She asked for a gin and tonic and went to sit beside Christopher. 'I kept getting lost,' she told him conspiratorially, as if that was the most exciting thing that had happened to her in the last hour; but she felt like a Judas.

'I should have fetched you, but I'm afraid I got talking, first with Jon and then with Jaydev again,' he apologised.

Thank God! Her forgiving smile was strained and it was a relief when Jaydev brought her drink over and raised his own glass, saying, 'Welcome once again to my home, Cadence, and to you both, long life and prosperity and as happy a marriage as I have. It's a pity the children were already in bed when you arrived, but you'll see them tomorrow. You too, Christopher. Pratap is seven now and Anjuna five. She was little more than a baby when you saw her last, I think.' He threw his wife a teasing glance and addressed the others, 'You wouldn't think a woman as innocent as Padmini has just proved herself to be a wife and mother, would you?'

'Oh, I'm slow rather than innocent, Jaydev. I've worked it out now,' Padmini declared laughingly.

There was further repartee, gradually giving way to the shared reminiscences of the four old friends, and Cadence didn't think anyone noticed that she was quieter than usual. Clearly there was a strong bond between the Nayars, and she just wished Christopher's other friend could have been as openly uncomplicated and likeable as Jaydev.

Christopher. She looked at him. It was classically ironical. He had brought her to India to meet his best friend, and the inevitable had happened. The tragedy was that she could never share the irony with him, and he would never guess at it either, being Christopher, her beautiful, beloved, trusting Christopher—whom she had so nearly betrayed.

ABODE OF PRINCES

о на сеттень учиния силу на станок ина зарежа спата,
ба кайни асалы плата ой а вна. Насти каннан кит
вна наменнина, казана задыкай с (факи перезаляй
ста као на неменнити

CHAPTER FOUR

A PEACOCK, gorgeously coloured, strutted on the
lawns, his drab harem in his wake, and at the end of
the immaculately mown sweep of green a formal lotus
pool shimmered in the heat-hazed morning light,
creamy-white, pink-tinted blossoms a soft blaze of
pastel colour. The cacophony of sound that Cadence
had come to associate with India was muted here, out
of town; instead there was birdsong, the soft voices of
servants and the occasional indignant rise in the tones
of Pratap and Anjuna Nayar as they disagreed about
something, playing beyond the lotus pool, having
breakfasted earlier.

Dressed in lemon yellow shorts, a brief white and
yellow top with a drawstring waist and the sandals she
had purchased in Bombay, Cadence sat opposite
Christopher at a table beneath one of the filigreed
stone arches that ran the length of the long shaded
verandah, supported by ornately carved pillars.
Behind them, the wide doors of the comfortable
breakfast-room stood open, discreet servants stationed
there ready to dart to the service of the guests at the
flicker of an eye. It was a comfortable, modern room
in complete contrast to the banqueting hall in which
they had dined the previous night. That, with its
domed ceiling inlaid with traditional mirror work that
reflected and refracted the light and broke up the
movements of those below into a strange wild
choreography, and its great white marble panels,
filigreed at the borders and inlaid with pale green
Indian jade, dark green malachite, mother of pearl and

smoky agate, had been awe-inspiring. The breakfast-room with its very Western sideboard bearing brass and sandalwood ornaments was somehow reassuringly familiar, but Cadence and Christopher had opted for the verandah.

Oppressed by guilt and frustration, Cadence had slept badly, but she had been up at her usual early hour, determined to work herself into what she thought of as a holiday mood. Putting off breakfast until Christopher, who slept late whenever he got the chance, was ready to join her, she had left Padmini presiding over the children's breakfast and taken herself off for a walk in the grounds, the marigold garland with which the small, adorable Anjuna had presented her about her neck.

The grounds were extensive, the guests of the hotel part of the palace having access to them, but an ample section had been retained for the exclusive use of the Nayar family. Cadence had walked as far as the *samand*, a large artificial lake created by one of Jaydev's forebears, and had been amused to discover that outside too, servants were constantly popping up to direct her, point out things of interest, answer her questions, and she wondered a little just how large a staff the Nayars employed. They certainly seemed to have created a great many jobs and as the palace was in a sense a national monument, it needed constant, caring maintenace. She supposed the fate of the palaces was not unlike that of the stately homes that had been opened to the public at home; the Indian princely families too were making the best of things.

One of the servants had pointed out to her the quarters where Colonel Nayar stabled his polo ponies and the field where games were played, but she had seen Jon and Jaydev arriving as she approached, so she had turned in another direction before they noticed her, inadvertently entering that portion of the grounds belonging to the hotel where, somewhat to her horror, she had met a man with some snakes in baskets. He had invited her to place a bet on an event scheduled for that afternoon, a fight to the death, when he intended to release a snake in the presence of a mongoose.

Finally, she had returned to the private wing of the palace to find Christopher up and looking for her, and now here they were, breakfasting on a tempting array of fruits, with servants ready to supply them with any other style of breakfast, should they want it.

'So he played for one of the snakes and it began to sort of weave about, but when he realised I didn't have any money on me to give him, he quickly shut it up in its basket again,' Cadence was describing her small adventures to Christopher.

'Yes, he would,' Christopher confirmed rather absently, and she realised that he was particularly quiet this morning. 'Cady, you didn't happen to see Jon while you were out, did you?'

'No. I mean yes.' Cadence's look was faintly haunted. 'But not to speak to. He and Jaydev were going to look at the polo ponies.'

'Oh, yes, Jaydev is trying to arrange a game for next week.' He paused. 'Cadence?'

'Yes?' She jumped guiltily at his serious tone.

'What's wrong?' he asked quietly.

'Christo . . .' Stricken, she didn't know what to say.

He sighed. 'You and Jon really don't get on, do you? He had virtually nothing to say . . . I tried to speak to him before dinner last night.'

'Yes, I know,' she admitted incautiously, ashamed of the relief she felt because he hadn't guessed the truth. 'He was angry with me for discussing it with you.'

'So I only made things worse,' Christopher realised sadly. 'I thought there was something. You were so unusually subdued at dinner last night.'

'I didn't think you'd noticed.' Her voice was almost a whisper.

He smiled slightly. 'I notice everything about you, my love. Oh, Cadence, I'm really sorry. I was only trying to help.'

'I know,' she said gently.

Another sigh escaped him, rueful and resigned. 'I suppose I was kidding myself all along. I assumed the two of you had to like each other, simply because it meant so much to me, but I realise it was inevitable that you would clash. You're so terribly alike.'

'Jon and me! Alike?' Startled and indignant, Cadence sat up straight, staring at him with something like horror, and he laughed.

'I don't suppose either of you will ever admit it if you really can't stand each other, but it's true. You're both so ... so very much alive, somehow, more so than other people. It's as if each of you has an abnormally strong life force. It flows out of you, like an electric current, and when it hits other people it shocks them. It's tangible, and visible too. People always notice you, and it's not just because you're two very good-looking people; it's more your sheer vitality they notice ... It's like a flame. I remember my father once saying it made him tired just to look at Jon sometimes, and then recently he said exactly the same thing about you. You'd been working all day and I'd fetched you and we had gone over to my parents' place. My mother was working in her garden and you immediately joined in, digging, weeding, watering, planting.'

'I just like gardening,' Cadence told him dismissively, still incensed at hearing she and Jon were alike; and that was true: her parents had turned their small garden over to her completely and in recent months she had put in a considerable amount of work in Stephanie Iverson's large, imaginative garden.

'So do a lot of people, but they don't all have your energy for it,' he countered teasingly. 'Calm down, Cadence, I'm just pointing out why I've now realised that you and Jon had to clash.'

'I hoped you wouldn't find out,' she confided regretfully.

'So did Jon, apparently. It was kind of you both to consider me, but unnecessary. I'm not a child who has to be protected from the truth. I can take it.'

And the other truth? The ensuing silence was extended as Cadence struggled with a confusion of feelings, among which shame was preponderant.

Finally she looked up at him. 'I'm sorry, Christo, desperately sorry. You must be so disappointed in me . . . in us both.'

He reached out to touch her hand, then looked up. 'Hullo, Jon!'

Cadence's glance flew to Jon's face to find it dark with fury, his eyes glittering with barely contained rage which seemed likely to erupt at any moment, and it was directed at her alone. He looked as if he could strike her, or strangle her, and in the same split second that she was absorbing all that, she was realising that having overheard her last words to Christopher, he must think she had just concluded a full confession of what had occurred last night.

Almost imperceptibly, she gave a negative sideways movement of the head, holding his gaze, willing him not to say anything, heaving an unconscious sigh of relief as she saw the rage die out of him as he comprehended her silent, desperate message.

The crisis had lasted no more than a couple of

seconds, and Christopher didn't seem to have noticed as he continued, 'I suppose you had breakfast hours ago? Cadence has also been up for hours . . . She says she saw you at the stables with Jaydev . . . I was just saying to her that you and she have got so much in common, and that's probably why you haven't taken to each other.'

Cadence bit the inside of her lower lip. Kindly, Christopher was indicating that there was no need for them to go on pretending, but the lie remained and she felt like a criminal. She wondered if Jon too was stricken by a sense of shame.

'I wouldn't have thought we had much in common, Christopher,' retorted Jon.

Christopher grinned. 'Cadence's reaction exactly. You're very alike.'

'What an appalling thought!'

'Isn't it?' Cadence joined in sweetly, a new game, a new pretence, to cover the truth, now that the old one had been ripped away, and yet not so much of a pretence. They might desire each other, but their mutual hostility was real.

'I didn't see you earlier. Why didn't you join us?' Jon asked her.

'I was avoiding you,' she admitted candidly, and both men laughed.

'That's our Cadence,' Christopher commented with humorous pride. 'Always truthful.'

'I've noticed,' drawled Jon. 'Terrifyingly so. I sometimes wonder how far she'll go, in her passion for honesty.'

'Have I hurt your feelings, Jon dear?'

'No——'

'You haven't any, I suppose!'

'But there are those whom your candour could wound.'

'More sensitive souls than you?' She held his gaze and gave him a brilliant smile. 'But I'm always kind to those I like, you see.'

'And those you love?' He was oddly persistent, and she realised the reassurance he sought.

'Well, obviously,' she snapped.

Christopher laughed quietly. 'You see, that's much better! You're enjoying yourselves now, like this, and you weren't before with all the politeness and pretence.'

'Careful, Christopher, you're starting to sound like what's-her-name—that child who kept looking on the bright side,' Jon laughed. 'But all right, I'll tell you. Cadence and I had a hell of a fight the morning you arrived in Bombay——'

'Don't exaggerate!' Cadence broke in, outraged.

'In the coffee shop,' he went on, casting her a taunting smile. 'We agreed that we didn't like each other—it was the only thing we did agree on!'

'Don't listen to him, Christo. He's making it sound as if we were throwing crockery around. We sat down and discussed it rationally.' Cadence's eyes sparkled challengingly.

'Is that what you call it? I never detected much rationality in what you were saying, but be that as it may, the outcome, Christopher, was that we decided you'd be upset and so, for your sake, we would try to behave in a civilised manner, but you're absolutely right, this is infinitely preferable, and living a lie came very hard to Cadence.'

And still did, she thought achingly.

'I can imagine,' Christopher agreed innocently. 'I'm glad you've got it all sorted out.'

'Right,' Jon agreed abruptly. 'Now, what are your plans? I ask because Sashi Kapur rang while you were still asleep. He has a couple of days free before his next

Iverson tour begins, and he'd like to see you. As I
didn't think you'd want to stir much today—you've
got nearly six weeks for running around after all—I
told him to come on over, about mid-morning, but I
said you'd ring and confirm it. All right?'

'Fine. I'm looking forward to seeing him again.'
Christopher looked at Cadence. 'Sashi is absolutely
the best of our Rajasthan guides.'

'I think you'll find the new girl pretty impressive
too,' commented Jon. 'And impressively pretty.'

'Sunila?' Christopher enquired guilelessly.

'Sunila,' Jon confirmed.

They were smiling at each other, that man-to-man
smile that shuts out women, but Cadence didn't mind.
It was a chance to observe the buddy-buddy
phenomenon which was beginning to fascinate her
where once she had tended to be rather scornful. It
made a difference when you knew the people involved,
and she was starting to realise that the bonds of
friendship between these two men were real and
strong. Although Jon was the older, dominant
character, and far more cynical and less trusting than
Christopher, he never gave any indication of despising
the younger man, and she liked him for that.

And she did like him, Cadence thought again with a
small shock. This way, the way he was this morning,
she liked and understood Jon Steele. He could amuse
her, and she had enjoyed that exchange with him just
now.

She looked at him and once again the sharp sweet
kick of desire assailed her, making her fingers and toes
curl, and beneath the table she pressed her knees
together in a way that would have been very revealing
to an expert on body-language.

He was such an incredibly beautiful man. Colouring
had a lot to do with it, the golden-brown skin, dark

hair and blazingly blue eyes, but now Cadence found herself looking at other things, interpreting them. There was that mouth for instance, sensual, cynical and a little cruel, but there was something else too, something she couldn't identify by word, but which softened her resentment and left her even more vulnerable than before. Too, there was the strength implicit in his jaw, the nose, definitely somewhat arrogant, she decided, and the hard planes of his face. It was a man's face. There was nothing of a boy there, and she remembered Stephanie Iverson telling her about a boy with a man's eyes. How long ago had that been? Twenty-five years, she worked it out, and was suddenly appalled. What hope was there, after all that time, what hope of any softness, any innocence? He had been a man all that long time, and he was only thirty-five!

These were dangerous thoughts and Cadence cut them off as soon as she realised it, transferring her attention to Christopher.

'As for our plans, we'll have to discuss them,' he was saying. 'I know Cadence wants to see as much of Rajasthan as possible in the time we've got. I know you've got work to do, but I hope we'll have you with us, Jon?'

'Give me a couple of days, and Jahanara and I should have reached a stage when I can legitimately take a break.'

'How's it going?'

Jon shrugged. 'Pretty well, though there's a lot of work in this one. As you know, I spent some time travelling around the country before coming here to take up Jaydev's offer of peace and quiet and space. I suppose I could have gone home, but I didn't want to lose the atmosphere, the sound of Indian voices, the feel of the air ... And it's easier if I have to go back anywhere to check on something. But as I say, I'm due for a break; I timed it this way when I knew you were coming, so ... If Cadence thinks she can bear my company?' Sardonic blue eyes rested on Cadence's face.

'The question is, can you?' she returned pleasantly.

The eyes grew wary, almost suspicious, but finally he said drily, 'Oh, I think I'll be able to ... endure.'

'Strong-minded, aren't we?' retorted Cadence, her smile limpid. But they shouldn't be doing this, she reflected hysterically, speaking about one thing and knowing Christopher thought they spoke of something else. It wasn't fair to Christopher.

'Let's hope so,' drawled Jon, glancing at his watch. 'I must leave you. Jahanara will be here in a minute. Incidentally, her brother—Hanif Khan—invited us three for dinner when I saw him last night. Does tomorrow night suit you? Right, I'll let Jahanara know. See you later.'

Halfway through the morning, Sashi Kapur arrived, a slender, attractive young man to whom Cadence took an instant liking which seemed to be reciprocated.

He, Christopher and Cadence sat talking Iverson Travel in an enclosed courtyard which had once been the secret garden of the ladies of the *zenana*. A fountain, surrounded by four smaller ones, played in the middle of the central raised garden, and channels of running water segmented the formal arrangement of flowers and greenery, while the outer perimeter was paved. It must have been a reaction to the desert land outside that had made previous maharajas include so many reminders of water at their palace, what with the samand, lotus pools and fountains, Cadence reflected, or perhaps it had been a status symbol, a way of flaunting their wealth.

Padmini had been with them earlier, while they had iced tea, but she had gone away afterwards, to oversee luncheon preparations as a business colleague of Jaydev's was expected, while Jon and Jahanara were shut up in the study that had been provided for Jon.

'I ought to be going,' Sashi stated some time later, and Cadence was surprised to discover more than an hour had passed in talking shop since Padmini's departure.

'I'll see you when the next trip is over, then, and we must also arrange some sort of social get-together soon,' said Christopher, getting to his feet. 'But before you go, let me go and get you one of those new brochures I was telling you about. I won't be a minute.'

Sashi smiled at Cadence as Christopher disappeared. 'I didn't realise until this morning that you also worked for Iverson Travel, Cadence. We had heard Christopher was engaged, of course, but not that it was to . . . one of the family, as it were. They're a good firm to work for, I think?'

'The best,' Cadence agreed emphatically. 'I wonder how I'd enjoy your job, though, on the move, backwards and forwards all the time. Do you ever meet your fellow guides, or do you all keep missing each other? The scheduling is pretty complicated, I know—it's part of the exam I have to write when we get home.'

Sashi's face had grown dark and sad. 'It can be difficult. I think that's partly why things didn't work out for Sunila and me.'

'Sunila de Souza?' Cadence was suddenly alert.

'Yes. She was my girl, you understand. I hoped to marry her. I thought she wanted it too, but then there was a phase when we kept missing each other, and then finally when we were both free at the same time,

I learnt that she was seeing Jon Steele.' He heaved a sigh. 'I can't blame her, I suppose. He's different, exciting and glamorous, and she was probably flattered when he became interested in her. He's a personality, good-looking and wealthy, and my Sunila is a very human girl. That's why I care so much about her, you see.'

'But . . .' Cadence couldn't understand the leaden ache in her breast. The anger in her mind was easier to comprehend, and it was a fierce, burning thing; she was almost literally seeing red. 'How could he do that, simply move in and take over another man's girl-friend? How could even Jon Steele do that?'

Especially when his affair with Sunila was intended as a temporary thing, as she had learned, but she didn't want to distress Sashi by saying so. He was upset enough already.

'Well, I don't suppose he knew about me,' he said sadly. 'I don't think she would tell him.'

'And didn't you say anything? To him?' she demanded.

'Where would be the point?' Sashi shrugged. 'By the time I found out it was too late. Anyway, he's not the sort of man you can go to and say "Give me back my girl." He'd have laughed at me . . . No, Sunila made her choice, but I'm so afraid, so afraid that one day he will drop her and what will she be left with, what will she have?'

'You?' Cadence suggested gently, her eyes compassionate. 'Will she still have you, Sashi?'

'She may not want me,' he said pessimistically before making a visible effort to cheer up. 'I don't know why I'm boring you with this, Cadence. I don't normally talk about it, but you have something, an air . . . You listen and I think you understand. All the same, I apologise most profusely.'

'No problem.' Cadence had picked up the phrase all India used. 'Here's Christo back.'

'Here you are, Sashi. I've just seen Padmini, Cadence; she says lunch in half an hour.'

'Then I'd better swop these shorts for something a bit less casual, if Jaydev is having a colleague in.' She turned to Sashi, her smile warm. 'Goodbye, Sashi, and good luck. See you again soon.'

'I'll come out with you, Sashi,' said Christopher.

Trying to find her way to the stairs leading to her room, Cadence passed through a richly carpeted hall containing several mysterious doors and off which three passages led, and as she did so, Jon Steele emerged from one of the rooms.

Eyes flashing and head held high, Cadence swept past him, but his voice arrested her:

'If you're looking for the way to your room, you're going the wrong way.'

'Thank you,' she said bitingly, turning and swinging past him once more.

Again he stopped her, this time with a hand on her arm, roughly turning her to face him.

'Now what?' he wondered sharply. 'What's wrong?'

Cadence glared at him contemptuously as she freed her arm with a jerk, revelling in being able to hate him again.

'Do you know, this morning I was in danger of actually liking you? Thank God it's passed. I think you're despicable, Jon. Stealing another man's girl-friend! I think——'

'What?' He looked blank.

'Sashi Kapur.'

'Sashi?' He was still incredulous.

'No, you don't know, do you?' she remembered scathingly. 'Sunila de Souza, Jon, the girl you've told Christo about, the girl you laugh about, all you men, you and Christo and Jaydev. But how do you think Sashi feels——'

'I didn't know,' he said flatly, his face suddenly taut and tired. 'She didn't tell me.'

'No, she wouldn't.'

'Why the hell didn't Sashi say something, speak to me?'

'That's right, blame someone else,' taunted Cadence. 'He didn't tell you because you're not the sort of man people can talk to. He was afraid you'd laugh.'

'No, people don't tell me things,' he agreed, his mouth twisting. 'They're all afraid of me.'

Cadence hesitated, torn, because she had enough sensitivity to imagine the loneliness such a fact must create, a cutting off from the rest of humanity.

But she didn't want to soften; she held on to her anger, challenging, 'And if he had told you, would it have made any difference, would you have cared? I don't think you care about anyone except yourself and your own selfish gratification. That's what you were about last night, wasn't it? You knew then, you didn't need any telling there, but you still went ahead——'

'As I recall, you were as involved as I,' he interrupted cuttingly.

'I was the one who stopped it,' Cadence retorted. 'And what about Sunila's feelings? Have you thought about that? You're planning to end it, aren't you? You've already nearly been unfaithful to her. How do you think she is going to feel when it's all over and she realises she's thrown away a possible lasting relationship with a nice man who really loves her for a brief fling with you?'

'I had no idea you Iverson Travel people felt so much loyalty towards each other,' drawled Jon. 'But you don't need to concern yourself over Sunila. She's known right from the beginning that there was a time-limit to our affair. She accepted it.'

'Probably because the poor girl was infatuated with you. All the same, I'll bet she regrets it bitterly when it's over.'

'Yes. Didn't Christopher ever warn you about me, Cadence? I hurt people.' His mouth twisted ironically. 'Even when I don't mean to, I hurt people.'

Again, she was stirred by his words, the un-compromising self-knowledge they betrayed; she felt herself yielding; she even lifted a hand, wanting to reach out, make contact, and for those moments the impulse had little to do with the sexual attraction between them.

But Cadence dropped her hand, before Jon had even noticed. She couldn't afford this sort of softening towards him. She didn't know why she was so sure of it, but from somewhere deep within her, where she knew herself and was beginning to know Jon Steele, came the conviction: to let herself weaken, to yield to feelings such as liking, or sympathy, was fully as dangerous as the physical desire they felt for each other.

So she only said, lightly, 'Yes, I believe Christo did mention something of the sort.'

Jon's smile was mirthless. 'Yes. He understands.'

'Well, I don't,' she retorted pointedly. 'I mean, how can he understand you, and still admire you? Because he does, you know. It's beyond me. You don't even try to live up to his admiration, do you?'

'I'm keeping my hands off you, am I not?' Jon countered sardonically.

'For his sake? And what's so noble about that?' Cadence mocked delicately. 'I don't flatter myself and Christopher that it's the great sacrifice of your life. You're a mature, adult man with plenty of experience, not a boy who has just discovered the candy jar and keeps wanting another taste, and another ... You must have some practice in controlling your physical urges, or haven't you? Do they all fall over backwards for you, like poor Sunila de Souza?'

'And you, Cadence?' he derided. 'You talk as if you too possess some considerable experience, so why do I get the impression that it's all just words?'

'I may not have your experience, but I'm not stupid and I'm not immature. People don't die of desire unfulfilled, and the only suffering is a kind of physical frustration. For that matter, I'm keeping my hands off you, but I'm not fool enough to think it's the hardest thing I'll ever have to do in my life. There'll be worse.'

Jon's face had hardened and he regarded her with something like contempt.

'You're so very sure of yourself, aren't you?' he challenged smoothly. 'You think you'll be able to go on resisting and resisting. I wonder if you realise how much that depends on my co-operation. As it is, we are in a sense on the same side, but if I were to change my mind, decide that I must have you, regardless ... I wonder how long you'd deny me ... how long you'd deny yourself, Cadence?'

Momentarily, she was stunned and breathless at the possibility, but she recovered, eyes flashing as she gave an angry laugh.

'It's what I might have expected of you! What does Christopher count for now, when you think your masculinity has been challenged? Let me tell you this, Jon—whatever gratification I might derive from going to bed with you, it couldn't be enough to compensate for the fact that I detest and despise you!'

'You talk like a child——'

'Oh, please!'

The small voice recalled them both and they swung round, Jon swearing. With her hair coiled into an elegant chignon today, and wearing straight glazed cotton trousers and a matching tunic top, Jahanara Khan stood trembling in the doorway of the room from which Jon had emerged a few minutes earlier, her distress palpable.

'I'd forgotten you were still in there,' Jon told her abruptly.

Jahanara's eyes were swimming. 'I'm so embarrassed. I tried coughing, and banging things about when you . . . When I realised, but you didn't seem to hear.'

Jon's laugh was harsh. 'No, we were both far too absorbed in each other,' he drawled.

'Don't worry about it, Jahanara,' Cadence tried to comfort her because the other girl looked really sick, a greenish-grey tinge marring her attactive dark face.

'But how can I help it?' Jahanara remained agitated. 'I heard you saying all those things, both of you, but you can't . . . you must not! What about Christopher? He would be so distressed if he knew. You can't hurt him like that!'

'I don't believe it!' Jon was grimly amused. 'Here's another one! What is it about Christopher, that we all feel this need to protect him? I know him better than either of you, and I know he's not some weakling who needs shielding from reality; he's a strong, well-balanced man who would rather face the truth than be lied to.'

'In this case it's a truth not worth telling because it won't always be the truth,' snapped Cadence. She looked at Jahanara more kindly, although she was starting to feel a slight sense of embarrassment at having been overheard. 'There's nothing to worry about, Jahanara. You heard what I said to Jon, that it wouldn't . . . be worth it. Christopher isn't going to be hurt. I care too much about him.'

And so do you, my girl, she added silently, giving Jahanara a last thoughtful look before leaving the hall. Jon she ignored completely.

CHAPTER FIVE

NEITHER Jon nor Christopher was likely to feel the slightest desire for her, looking the way she did now, Cadence reflected ruefully as she surveyed the crop of mosquito bites adorning her usually slenderly attractive ankles and upper arms.

They were the penalty she had to pay for a pleasant informal evening spent sitting out on the palace lawns, sipping gin and tonic and helping herself to vegetable pakora, with Jon, Christopher and the Nayars, and she was philosophical about them. As long as she remembered to take her malaria tablets and didn't scratch, no lasting harm would come of them.

But they weren't pretty. Vanity half-tempted her to conceal them by donning one of her punjabis, but it was so hot, and while Indian girls and women seemed to cover up against the heat, probably sensibly, Cadence found it difficult to break the Western habit of wearing as little as possible in hot weather.

That was why she was bra-less beneath the thin sleeveless top she had purchased locally. The short graceful skirt was of the same material and intricate print, brown and golden yellow and russet hand-printed with blocks on a creamy background, and she wore her Bombay sandals, already grown comfortable with much wear.

She had been resolute in refusing to allow the situation with Jon to spoil these first few days in Rajasthan, and she had not been disappointed. The abode of princes lived up to its romantic reputation, a desert state of endless fascination, studded here and

there with its legendary, different coloured cities as if
with jewels—the dark honey colour of the nearby city
over which Jaydev's forefathers had once ruled; the
lighter golden yellow stone of filigreed Jaisalmer, the
colour of the desert sand; the rose pink of Jaipur, the
state capital and the most Indian of Indian cities, it
was claimed; the reddish pink of Bikaner amid the
barren wilderness; pinkish-brown Jodhpur . . .

Cadence and Christopher had explored as the mood
took them, sometimes alone, sometimes accompanied
by Jon and Jahanara, or Jaydev and Padmini who had
put one of their cars permanently at their disposal.
Their evenings had been mostly spent relaxing at the
palace, save for the night when, accompanied by Jon,
they had dined with Jahanara and her brother, Hanif
Khan, a dark slim young man whose extreme good
looks were matched by his beautiful old-fashioned
manners.

Today, however, was different. They were to be a
proper foursome, she and Christopher, Jon and Sunila
de Souza, who was free for a few days and was
combining seeing her lover with reporting to her
English boss, having been invited to accompany them
to the deserted city of Amber, one of the places to
which she regularly escorted Iverson Travel's clients.

Picking up her sunhat and shoulder bag, Cadence
departed from her sumptuous room to go down and
wait for the men in the entrance hall, having left them
still at breakfast a few minutes ago. She paused in
crossing the huge space, her eyes caught by a little
figure in one of the sitting-rooms or waiting-rooms off
the hall, and hesitated, guessing who it was and torn
between reluctance to meet Sunila de Souza and a
natural curiosity about her.

Part of her, the physical part, the weak woman's
flesh that still craved Jon Steele, was already,

unreasonably but understandably, responsible for a dislike of the girl who had known the pleasures she must deny herself, while the rational, thinking Cadence whose compassion had been stirred by what she knew of the affair was afraid that she might convey, by a pitying look or some expression of concern, that she knew Sunila's days with Jon were numbered—and it was for Jon to break it to her, and no one else.

The petite figure turned as she stood hesitating there, and came skimming out into the hall. She was clad in a simple cotton sari over a plain v-necked top that left her midriff bare, but an aristocratic Indian physiognomy had been overlaid with the passionate face of Latin Europe, making her quite exquisite, a doll-like little creature with huge dark eyes thickly lashed, a sensual mouth and glossy dark curls that danced about the small, perfect face they framed as she moved.

'Good morning! Miss Reay? It has to be!' The lilting voice was as enthusiastic as her glowing face, and she held out a hand.

'Cadence.' Smiling, because it was impossible not to, impossible not to like this adorable child, Cadence shook hands.

'Sunila de Souza.'

'I've heard a lot about you.'

Sunila giggled. 'I can imagine. Oh, dear!'

'But we were expecting to pick you up on our way to Amber.'

'I know, darling, but then I heard of someone who was driving out this way, and I thought I'd save you the trouble and surprise Jon, so here I am! And where are the men? I see you're all ready to go ... It is we who should keep them waiting! Conventionally, anyway. Have you got your camera?' She laughed. 'Oh

dear! I'm so used to it now, it has become a habit—
being a guide. Cadence, I am just thrilled to meet you
and so looking forward to meeting Mr Iverson junior.
But nervous too, of course!'

'Nervous of Christopher?' Cadence couldn't help
smiling.

'Well, after all, he is my boss,' Sunila explained in
her prettily emphatic way. 'I spoke to him on the
telephone last night, and he said I could say my piece
at Amber ... Is he a perfectionist, tell me? Very
demanding, very particular? Oh, I'm good at my job, I
have a lot of self-confidence, and the tourists like me,
but ... Cadence, can I ask you a tremendous favour?
Please! When Mr Iverson junior asks me to tell him
about Amber, will you go away a bit and take Jon with
you? I don't mind a crowd of tourists, but when Jon
looks at me, I can't concentrate. It's ... it's
distracting! Will you?'

'I'm not sure ...' Cadence hesitated.

'Please!'

'Oh, all right!' laughed Cadence. It was always so
hard to say no to charming children, when they asked
so nicely.

'Oh! But Mr Iverson junior might expect you to be
there, will he? Someone told me you also work for
Iverson Travel,' Sunila remembered concernedly.

'It's all right. Incidentally, I think you could call
him Christopher. Sashi Kapur does.' Cadence brought
the name in deliberately, curious as to what the
reaction might be, but Sunila's expression didn't
change.

'I think I'd better wait until he invites me
personally. Sashi has met him before, you see. What
exactly is your position in Iverson, Cadence?'

'Well, I was head of one of the branch agencies, but
when we go home I'm due to sit an exam which, if I

pass, will mean that I become a tour co-ordinator. Of course, it's all done by telex, and I'll lose the contact with the public, but it is promotion,' Cadence conceded.

'I think I'd like that. I wonder, if I ever went to London ... Oh, dear, I talk too much!' Sunila broke off, giggling self-consciously, and then, as Jon, Christopher and Jaydev appeared at the far end of the hall, her cheeks grew rosy and a shyly excited sparkle appeared in the dark eyes as she gazed at Jon and didn't seem to notice the other two.

She's only a baby, Cadence thought angrily, her mouth tightening, and her own eyes, as they met Jon's, were as cold as she could make them—but it wasn't easy. She knew exactly what Sunila meant about the distracting qualities of those blazing eyes.

Jon's face tautened as he read her expression, relaxing only as he gave his attention to Sunila, bending his head—to kiss her? That Cadence didn't want to see and she turned to Christopher and Jaydev with a haste that impaired her usual grace.

'Have a wonderful, wonderful day, my friend,' Jaydev was saying. 'Are you sure you don't want a driver?'

His words went echoing round Cadence's mind long after they were on their way in the pleasantly air-conditioned car, but now they rang with a hollow mockery in place of the cheerful goodwill with which their host had invested them.

How could they, any of them, hope for a wonderful day? The four of them were a bad mix, a crazy mix, a dangerous mix. There were too many currents and how could they remain hidden beneath the surface when they had such a power to disturb? Secret desire, planned cruelty, the temptation to betrayal ... And she had made that stupid promise to Sunila, to take

Jon away for a while when her first allegiance should be to Christopher, and that meant avoiding being alone with Jon.

To that end, she had had his co-operation in the last few days, and she suspected that Jahanara Khan too was playing her part in protecting Christopher's interests as she had become a decidedly duenna-like presence lately, but as to her reasons for doing so, Cadence felt more concern than gratitude.

The ruined city of Amber itself was wonderful, though, the massive palace spread over the long hillside and the Jaigarh fortress above reflected in the long lake below.

In her eagerness to see it close up, Cadence was ahead of the others, a small beggar at her heels. 'Chocolate? Smarties?' he made the request she kept hearing, and when she didn't answer him, he tried a few basic phrases of German and Spanish, and she wanted to laugh because he had been enterprising enough to learn them.

'What's your hurry?' Jon was at her side suddenly and he addressed the urchin in one of India's many, many dialects—Cadence still couldn't differentiate between any of them.

'What did you say to him?' she asked.

'Roughly—beat it.' His lips twitched.

'The little ones amaze me,' she confided. 'Their persistence. Yesterday afternoon when Christo and I went into town, he was virtually forced to have his shoes cleaned because this little boy kept darting after him wherever he moved, taking swipes at his shoes. Eventually he felt such persistence merited some co-operation, so he stood still, and the child proceeded to polish and polish away for . . . oh, it must have been a good ten minutes. Christo was starting to think he meant to get through to his feet!'

'At least that one was working for his rupees,' Jon laughed.

'It's altogether an incredible country, this!'

'Yes.' He was thoughtful. 'It can arouse pity, but if you yield to every sight that evokes it, you'd soon be bankrupt. But it can also kill pity.'

'How?'

'One can become inured, seeing so much suffering that a hardening of such impulses inevitably occurs. What will it do to you, Cadence, I wonder?'

'It arouses stronger emotions than pity—respect or admiration, I'm not sure what the right word is. When you think of all the tragedy and conflict of the recent past, and then you keep meeting Indians for whom there is no conflict, to whom someone of another creed is just another fellow-Indian ... I'm not explaining it very well, I know, but——'

'I know what you mean,' Jon said quietly.

'And you, Jon?' Why did she want to know him, to understand him? It was so dangerous.

'It's different for me,' he answered slowly. 'I've always felt that part of me ... belonged here. I lost myself among India's millions for a time, as a boy, and there were those who ... helped me on my way, fed me, hid me, advised me. I thought of them as my people.'

Stephanie told me about that time.' Cadence looked at him. 'Why did you do it?'

'I don't know.' He shook his head, eyes looking inward. 'I suppose ... because I didn't want to be sent to England. I'd known so few Western people, apart from my parents. We spent most of our time in Asia or Africa, I'd attended schools with the local kids ... Europe was strange to me.'

'You were lucky in the family you went to,' she ventured softly.

'Yes.' Suddenly his face was shuttered as he glanced at her. 'There's no need for reminders of how much I owe the Iversons, sweetheart.'

'I wasn't ... It wasn't a reminder.' Involuntarily, she put a hand to his arm, but he flinched away from the contact. 'I don't think they feel you owe them anything, Jon. What they gave you was freely given.'

He laughed faintly. 'Don't you think that makes it even worse? It's a debt I can never repay, because they put no price on it. Good people, as the Iversons are, can destroy with their goodness, their kindness ...'

'No! How can you view it like that?' Cadence was genuinely shocked, a crease of perplexity appearing between her eyebrows as she stared at him. 'Do you really not know what it was that they gave you, Jon? Not kindness ... It was love, and they believe you love them too. Stephanie told me that ... Or is that it? Don't you love them? Can't you? Is that——'

'I don't think you really understand what I'm talking about, so let's just drop it, shall we?' Jon cut in distantly. 'Shall we slow down and wait for the other two?'

Disappointed, she was about to protest, but then the colourful scene ahead distracted her.

'Elephants, Jon!' Again she touched his arm, this time in a gesture meant to communicate her pleasure, wanting to share it with him, and he turned on her with a look of such violent resentment that she took a hasty step away from him.

'For God's sake, will you stop doing that!' he demanded savagely, voice low and intense, almost a whisper. 'I was right about you in Bombay. I thought then that you were as innocently lethal as a young lioness, and you are. You just haven't got a clue, have you?'

'I'm sorry,' Cadence hissed back, as Christopher
and Sunila reached them.

She realised then that she actually needed to keep
touching him, and not only in a sexual context. She
wanted to be close to him, understand him. She
needed to be in contact, mentally and physically;
even in Christopher's presence she needed it because,
she realised with bitter shame, all those complex
desires carried more wieght than her loyalty to
Christopher—more weight even than her love for
Christopher.

'What's wrong?' asked Christopher, noticing their
faces. 'Are you quarrelling again?'

'Cadence was just getting somewhat excited about
the elephants and I wasn't at my most sympathetic,'
Jon claimed ironically. 'Of course, as it's your first
visit to Amber, you must ride up the hill, Cadence.'

'Not without Christopher!' she protested instantly,
and Christopher laughed.

'He's teasing, my love. It's a long, hot, steep walk,
so we'll all ride up. Sunila has promised to engage her
favourite mahout.'

The elephants carried four plus the mahout, and the
ride up the hill was another of the new experiences
which always appealed so strongly to Cadence's love of
novelty. So was the blessing she and Sunila received in
a temple at the top, so devoutly Hindu that not only
shoes had to be removed, but all leather articles must
be left outside, bags, belts, camera cases, watchstraps.
The men declined to join them, and Cadence
wondered whimsically what that indicated about their
characters and if they felt themselves sufficiently
blessed already. Later, however, with a vermilion
smudge on her forehead and seeing the one on
Sunila's, she decided it had merely been vanity: they
didn't want to walk around with marks on their faces.

At least it was more colourful than the smudge you got on Ash Wednesday, though, she thought.

They strolled about the crumbling palace together for a time, and although it was evident that Sunila was completely at ease and confident with Christopher by now, Cadence nevertheless kept her promise to her when she heard Christopher kindly request some information about Amber's history—and she knew she was doing it more for her own sake than for Sunila's: she wanted to be alone with Jon Steele.

Somehow, it came as no surprise to discover that she could communicate her wishes to him without word or gesture. She simply looked at him, he looked back, and simultaneously they drifted away, up a broad flight of stairs, through a foliated arch and into another vast, sunlit courtyard.

Only then did Jon say, 'Why are we deserting?'

She laughed. 'Sunila wants to impress Christopher and she finds your presence distracting.'

'Ah, Sunila!' His smile was so indulgent that Cadence immediately felt intensely angry.

'What are you doing with a child like that, Jon?' she demanded. 'She's only a baby.'

'My dear Cadence, Sunila is twenty-one, exactly one year younger than you,' he drawled.

'Age has nothing to do with it,' she snapped. 'Nor has physical maturity. She's a child with stars in her eyes and dreams in her mind, and one of these days she's going to be disillusioned. You're even planning it, aren't you?'

Jon's expression was unyielding. 'She'll have only herself to blame. I warned her at the start. If she's forgotten what I said, or has hoped to change things, I don't think that's my fault.'

'No, of course not, but the fact that she was foolish won't stop her hurting, will it?'

'Then she shouldn't have been so stupid,' he retorted unfeelingly.

'All people are stupid when they're in love,' Cadence flared, appalled by his callousness. 'And she's in love with you. Did you expect her not to be?'

'I could have done without it, but truthfully, I didn't consider the possibility to begin with. I suppose I didn't care one way or the other,' he admitted.

'You really are a bastard, aren't you? You said I was lethal, back there, down the hill! Don't you know just how lethal you are? Have you never noticed the effect you must have on romantically minded girls like Sunila?'

She was still angry, yet it occurred to her that while she felt desperately sorry for Sunila, some of the concern causing her anger was on his behalf. Was she going completely insane? Jon had no need of it. What in the world was she concerned about? The salvation of his soul?

Jon was shrugging. 'All this confirms that the sooner I end it, the better.'

'I don't suppose you'll manage to do it kindly,' Cadence retorted waspishly.

'I'm not kind, remember?' His tone was silken. 'Tell me, Cadence, what makes you think you have the right to question me about my personal affairs?'

The strange thing was that, logically, she knew she had no right whatsoever, but at a deeper level, beyond the reaches of the intellect, she felt as if she had the right. Suddenly alarmed by the gathering complexity of her feelings where Jon was concerned, Cadence looked at him.

'Of course I have no right,' she conceded lightly, smilingly, aware now of the need to distance herself. 'I do apologise, Jon. Since I'm missing out on Sunila's expert's knowledge, you'll have to be my guide. Where are we now? This whole massive structure seems to be a series of palaces within a palace, and all with such labyrinthine ways. I can just imagine some poor newcomer, a servant or someone, getting lost and being found wandering days later, out of his mind and starving! They really built on a big scale in those days, didn't they?'

'They needed to,' commented Jon, smiling at the enthusiasm that had replaced what had begun as a mere conventional request aimed at restoring the impersonal to their conversation. 'What with the massive entourages they had then—ministers of state, servants, wives, children, harems, the lot! This is the zenana palace that we're entering now, and here especially you see the Moghul influence—the Amber rulers allied themselves to the Moghul emperors in Delhi—but the imagery, the peacocks, elephants and so on, is of course typically Hindu.'

'Yes, I noticed when we had dinner with Jahanara and Hanif that they had no imagery whatsoever in their home, not a single representation of any living creature, not even a picture or ornament depicting an animal, although Hanif clearly loves horses.'

'Islam is a very powerful influence. I would imagine there are far fewer apostates there than from any other faith.'

'And yet it seems less strange to me than some of the others—more like ours, with the same prophets we know, as Hanif pointed out.'

'Yes. I've heard this over and over again, about the days when the British were in India,' Jon told her. 'That while the administrative posts were filled by Hindus, the British made more personal friendships with Muslims because they were socially more at ease with them, especially when the caste system was still so widely adhered to by Hindus. A Muslim could and

would sit down and eat with you, a caste Hindu—
never! I suppose that's why so many Untouchables
were converted to Islam, there finding the acceptance
their own faith couldn't offer.'

Cadence was smiling to herself. She liked listening
to him because it really meant something to him; he
really cared and his interest was real; as he had said
earlier, part of him belonged here.

She liked listening to him, she liked sharing her
thoughts with him—quite simply she liked being with
him. As they wandered through the zenana quarters, it
occurred to her that he was actually happy in his
company, when they weren't quarrelling. She wanted
to be with him more than anything else in the world.

I'm engaged to Christopher, she thought with
sudden panic.

She looked at the ring on her left hand, symbol of
love and promise for the future, and an ache was
spreading round her heart. She thought about it a
while, examining the pain to see what it meant, and
she thought about right and wrong, and love and
loyalty, and truth and lies, but finally she had to
abandon it, confused and uncertain, unsure of
anything any more, where before she had been so very
sure. She only knew that the way to the once bright
future was shadowed, but whether she could pass
through those shadows and emerge untouched by
disaster was beyond her guessing.

The company and the place were not conducive to
self-analysis, anyway, and she had this little time to
spend legitimately with Jon. Why waste it in
introspection when it might be all she ever had?

'I'm glad, anyway, that I'm here today and not
then,' she reflected aloud, gazing thoughtfully round
the chamber in which they stood. 'I wouldn't like to
have been a woman in those days.'

'Oh, I don't know,' Jon responded lightly. 'The princesses and concubines lived a life of lazy luxury. See this contraption here. A giant hand-pulled fan or *punkah* would have hung from it, so for a start you'd have been cooler than you are here today; the furnishings and fabrics would have been infinitely beautiful and sinfully comfortable, you'd have lived a life of leisurely ease——'

'With nothing to do but await my husband's pleasure—if he'd bothered to marry me—and knowing that I shared him with dozens of other women. I'd have gone crazy with boredom!'

He looked at her assessingly. 'Yes, I believe you would, and it would have been a crime ... All that energy only being called on once in a while. Only you'd probably have been the favourite.'

'Well, thanks,' she laughed wryly. 'In which case, I wouldn't have lasted long. My life would have been in danger if some of Padmini's stories are true; some rival would have been plotting to supplant me. Think of the life, Jon! Having to observe strict purdah, having to watch everything that was going on from behind a window covered with grilled stonework, never being able to be a participant, quarrelling with the other women ... And at the end of it, not my end but my husband's, *sati*. Everywhere we've been in Rajasthan, we've seen those stone walls with their handprints, commemorating *satis*.'

'There was little alternative to *sati*—or *suttee*. A woman's life ended with her husband's or lover's. It was even a matter for rivalry, whether she got to share the chief pyre or one of the others. There were instances of over sixty wives and concubines following certain princes to the pyre, and committing the rite was also a sign of breeding in those times as it was usually confined to the higher castes.'

'So it was expected. I wonder if any of them ever did it for love.'

'Some, surely,' said Jon, surprising her since she had thought his cynicism total.

'I couldn't!' Cadence shuddered.

He smiled. 'You're a very modern girl, Cadence.'

'And Christopher wouldn't expect it,' she laughed.

'No.' He had stopped smiling. 'Let's move on, shall we?'

Another sunbaked courtyard awaited them, a few other people strolling about it. Jon paused and looked at her with something approaching irritation.

'You look a sight,' he told her brutally. 'Red smudge on your forehead, mosquito bites all over you ... And if you don't wear that hat instead of flapping it around all the time, you're going to look even worse. Sunburn isn't pretty.'

'Well, thanks,' she said sharply, wondering at his abrupt change of mood. 'But I don't burn, I tan. Anyway, Jon dear, I'm glad to know you're cured!'

'But I'm not,' he said, quietly and deliberately.

Cadence's mouth went dry. They stood looking at each other, heedless of the brilliant white Indian sunshine beating down on them, the place and the people forgotten. There were only Jon and Cadence, and an unendurable space between them.

She felt a great hot wave of desire engulfing her, and knew that he too was assaulted by something similar, a violence done to the senses by the call of blood to blood, flesh to flesh ... She stood as if in a soundless dream, perceiving him, all of him, with something beyond the mind, beyond even the senses, as if knowledge of him came to her through her pores, drawn in, as she was drawn in to his knowledge, and they became one person though a metre of space lay between them.

Cadence swayed, and Jon stirred and began to walk away, a look of intent on his face, so concentrated that he seemed blind to all but one purpose.

She followed. Neither of them said a word. There was no need. They both knew what was going to happen when he found what he sought, a place where they could be alone for a time.

Up winding stairs and along a narrow passages she followed him, to one of the upper floors of the circular stone structures adjoining some of the buildings in the complex that had once comprised a palace. The glassless windows, covered in stone filigree with a square hole in the middle, commanded a view of wild hills, but neither of them noticed.

Passion had exploded, a wild, savage passion that hurt as much as it pleasured, shot through as it was with desperation. They clung frantically together, mouths violently fused, bodies straining, limbs locked.

There was no relief, though, only a mounting frustration, unbearable, as heat gathered, more searing than the day outside, and desire leapt and leapt to intolerable heights. Frenziedly questing hands slid over burning, perspiration-dampened flesh, hips ground together, and still there was no release, no ease to be had, limited and confined as they were by the time and the place.

'Jon, Jon!' Cadence sobbed his name, faint with the need that quivered and leapt through all her being.

She felt him shaking against her as, groaning, he sought her mouth a second time, the intimacy of tongues twining endlessly together no substitute for the act that was denied them, but still exquisitely erotic, stoking their madness.

There was no door to the strange circular room. Cadence's bag and hat lay on the floor. If anyone had looked in, neither Jon nor Cadence would have noticed, lost in their paroxysm of passion that was so intense it was almost fighting of a sort, for they seemed to struggle both with and against each other, seeking, always seeking, for more, to be closer, closer than the barrier of clothes permitted.

Cadence was whimpering, wordlessly pleading for release from this crazed wanting that possessed her so utterly; soft sounds, low cries and little gasps that begged for the assuagement of the throbbing ache of hunger that was her hollow, unfulfilled womanhood.

Jon's hands moved on her, fierce, possessive, dominant, and yet out of control. They burnt through the thin Indian cloth of her garments, and she writhed in pained pleasure as hard seeking fingers possessed sensitive flesh, probed, moved on, turning her about, closing over the aching hardness of her breasts, swollen nipples thrust against the fabric.

'Oh, Cadence!' His voice a hoarse whisper, he dragged her up against the length of his hard shuddering body once more and she wound her arms about his neck, panting as his mouth moved to possess hers in another savage demand, roughly taking the wild sweetness of its response in the act that could never appease, never slake—it could only inflame their mutual, tearing need for the other, ultimate act.

Finally, however, Jon tore himself from her grasp, almost flinging her away.

Cadence leaned against the cool wall, afraid of fainting. She drew a long shuddering breath, expelled it, and went to retrieve her bag and sunhat. Her body felt bruised and unsated, still stingingly alive, passion still wildly stirring, but she knew as well as he that there could be no more.

Only when she straightened did she look at Jon again. His back to her, he stood at the filigreed window, a dark and rigid figure.

'Jon.'

She thought he sighed. 'I cannot, I just cannot take much more of this,' he said harshly.

'Jon . . ,' She didn't know what to say.

He turned to face her. 'No discussion, there's nothing to be said,' he snapped. 'Damn it, Cadence, you've got to persuade Christopher to make that planned trip to Kashmir soon, and take you with him . . . I've got to have some respite! I can't go on like this.'

'I'll try,' she promised quietly.

There was a short silence, then Jon said abruptly, 'We'd better find the others. Have you got make-up and a mirror in that bag?'

'Yes.' She busied herself, doing the best she could in the dim light, a little shocked by the sight of her face. The slightly swollen, inflamed lips were less noticeable with careful outlining and filling in, but there was nothing she could do about her pallor or the shame in her eyes.

When she looked at Jon, she saw that his face too told the story; his lips and face anyway, but it was not shame that she saw in his eyes—it was a bitterly angry frustration.

They found Christopher and Sunila near the entrance, watching some monkeys and their babies cavorting on a wall. Cadence looked at Jon as they approached.

'Christo will know if you look like that,' she said gently.

'I'm sorry, I can't help it,' he returned broodingly. 'And I couldn't help it.'

'And me with my mosquito bites and all,' she commented lightly because the effort had to be made for Christopher's sake. She was relieved when he smiled.

'I don't think I added to your number of bites, did I?'

Thus, they were laughing as they rejoined the others but, her eyes going to Jon's mouth once more, Cadence thought sadly: It's no use. Christo is going to know.

CHAPTER SIX

CADENCE still didn't know if Christopher knew or not, and she could hardly ask him in case he didn't.

After lunching in Jaipur with its famous chiselled Hawa Mahal, or Palace of Winds, in the old city, they had made the long drive back to the Nayars, bringing Sunila with them. She and Jon had gone for a walk, while Cadence and Christopher played with the Nayar children in the swimming pool that was a fairly recent addition, the large original palace pool now being for the use of the hotel guests.

Now, however, they were sitting in the shade of the verandah, still with Pratap and Anjuna in tow, discussing Kashmir. Christopher seemed in no hurry to arrange that business leg of his trip, and Cadence couldn't tell him why she thought he should be in a hurry.

'You can't go to Kashmir yet anyway,' Pratap joined in the discussion. 'My father has arranged that polo game, remember?'

'You're absolutely right, Pratap,' Christopher agreed. 'That settles it.'

'Perhaps I could go with you when you do go, though,' the boy went on hopefully. 'I should like to go to Kashmir.'

'You've got school,' Anjuna reminded him—she was extremely jealous of the fact. 'But I can go.'

'Somehow I don't think your parents will agree,' Christopher told them. 'What would you do all the time, anyway? I'm going on business.'

'I went on a business trip with my father once,' retorted Pratap. 'Boys should know about business.'

'And girls,' Anjuna insisted positively, looking for a quarrel.

Cadence studied Christopher as he gave his attention to the pair. Oh, dear God, did he know or didn't he? He didn't seem upset, he was his normal, gently agreeable self, but he had been quiet during the drive home and surely he must have noticed the tension that kept her and Jon equally quiet? Most of the talking had been done by a vivacious Sunila, elated with Christopher's praise of her abilities as an Iverson Travel guide and happy to be in her beloved Jon's company.

Did he know? The guilty question haunted her, and either way, what was she going to do? Perhaps if she and Christopher were to make love properly it would consolidate their relationship, reinforce her love for him. Then she wouldn't be tempted again . . .

But Cadence recognised the futility of that course, as well as the fact that she would be using Christopher and thereby cheating him as surely as she would if she yielded to the temptation Jon Steele presented.

And anyway, she didn't want to go to bed with Christopher—she couldn't, wanting Jon as she did. She still felt stunned when she thought of their almost ferocious lovemaking that morning, forced to admit that she had never been so utterly consumed when Christopher kissed her. She had never gone up in flames like that for him.

What am I going to do?

'What is it, Cady?' Christopher asked quietly, and for a moment she thought she had spoken aloud.

She put out a hand to touch his where it rested on the arm of his chair and was shocked to see that she was trembling. Even her smile felt wobbly, unreal—a lie!

She glanced at the children and mouthed silently, 'I love you.'

It was a ritual exchange in which they had occasionally indulged when in public, and he responded with a warm smile, but then his gaze was distracted by someone down at the lotus pool.

'Look at that, love. Sunila, in floods of tears, I think.'

'And she was so happy earlier! This is your friend's doing—I suppose you realise that?'

'It had to come,' he said gently. 'I hope she's all right. Will you see? I'll take the infants and myself off, or she'll be embarrassed. Pratap, how about looking in on the ponies now? You too, Anjuna.'

'But that lady there is crying!' Anjuna was clearly tempted to linger. 'Big people don't cry. Why is she crying?'

'Ladies do, they're just big girls really,' Pratap asserted scornfully as he and Anjuna were shepherded away, and Cadence laughed silently—there was a little chauvinist in the making! Then she went to meet Sunila.

Sunila was reacting dramatically.

'It's over—finished!' she declared, and cast herself into Cadence's arms which didn't quite work out since Cadence wasn't expecting it and staggered under the onslaught, but she managed to steady herself, patted a shoulder and then walked her to the verandah, sat her down and lent a sympathetic ear while Sunila sobbed out her misery.

Her distress was genuine and tragic, and Cadence felt desperately sorry for her, and even more so when the tears stopped and Sunila raised a wan and woebegone little face from which all the sparkle and vivacity was gone.

'I've been such a fool,' she whispered brokenly. 'I

knew, he warned me, but I loved him so . . . Oh, what
am I to do? What's to become of me now?'

A thought struck Cadence. 'Are you pregnant?'

'No, he made sure that there was no chance,' Sunila
answered distractedly. 'But oh, Cadence, how am I to
bear this? I love him . . . And I hate him too, now! I
threw away everything, and who will want me now?
There was a man, you know, who . . . who really loved
me.' She began to cry quietly again as if she had only
just realised the reality of that man's love as opposed
to Jon Steele's feelings. 'I was stupid, so stupid . . . I
neglected him for Jon! And now I've lost them both.'

'Not necessarily,' Cadence said gently, hoping she
was right. 'You're talking about Sashi Kapur, aren't
you? I've heard him mention you and I gained a
strong impression that he still felt . . . considerable
affection for you, Sunila. Perhaps, not now, but one
day, when the hell and the hurting aren't so bad . . .?'

'No! He will never forgive me, I know that!' Sunila
declared vehemently, apparently convinced that she
didn't deserve forgiveness either, although as Sashi
himself had said, she was only a very human girl.
'How could he? No, that sort of thing is over for me
now, for ever.'

Cadence did some quick thinking, decided that it
would serve more purpose to talk to Sashi than quote
him to Sunila, and proceeded to offer what comfort
she could, at the same time reassuring herself that
Sunila was not suicidal and that when not on the road
for Iverson she lived with her own large, loving
family.

Sunila was calmer by the time Christopher
reappeared, alone now, and she stood up, trying to
give him a smile. 'I really ought to be going now. Do
you think one of the drivers——'

'I'll drive you home,' said Christopher.

'No, that's all right, Jon said he'd arrange with one of the drivers. He wanted to drive me himself, but I never want to see him again. I suppose you know what has happened?' Sunila added.

'Yes—I'm sorry. Jon told me,' Christopher offered gently. 'And he asked me to do this, take you home. I know you're hurt, but he's not a total monster, Sunila, and he's concerned about you.'

Dark eyes flashed, very Latin then. 'I do not wish for his pity. No! If this is his arrangement, I will have nothing to do with it!'

'Let him do this last thing for you, Sunila.' Christopher smiled. 'And let me. You're still one of us, one of Iverson Travel, and we like to look after our staff. You're all important to us, and our guides are among the most important.'

Sunila looked thoughtful. 'Yes . . . my work. I have that still. It will be all I have. Thank you, yes, all right. Can we go now at once please?'

'Will you come with us, Cady?' Christopher wanted to know.

'I don't think so, darling. I have to wash my hair,' she excused herself with a faint smile, her honey eyes reassuring him that Sunila would be all right.

She also had to find out how and where to contact Sashi who was on the road at present, but first she saw them off. Then she went into the palace, encountering Padmini in one of the glittering halls.

'Have you seen Jon?'

'He's in the study he uses, I think,' Padmini told her, and Cadence set off, pleased to realise she was at last beginning to know her way round.

She knocked and entered in response to his summons. He was seated at an inlaid desk, notebooks strewn about him, and he looked up at her with weary resignation.

'I suppose you've come to ask me why I had to be so brutal and tell me again what a bastard I am,' he challenged tiredly, blue eyes sweeping her long legs and the slender curves of her body, now clad in chalk-coloured shorts and a soft coral vest.

Cadence closed the door before replying. 'Was it very difficult, Jon?'

He looked faintly surprised. 'Yes—yes, it was.' He pulled his mouth into a straight line. 'She cried, then she had a tantrum, then she pleaded with me—that was the worst—and finally she cried again. What are you doing, Cadence?'

'Nothing. It's all right,' she soothed.

She didn't know why she had done it—why she was doing it. As he spoke she had moved round to his side of the desk and now she stood beside his chair, one hand on his shoulder. It was all right, she knew. Sex was absent for now; she could offer comfort, sympathy, and he would not snap at her for arousing him.

'Contrary to what you may believe, I don't actually enjoy hurting people, you know,' he went on after a moment.

'I know.'

'I tried not to be too brutal.'

'What did you say? No, that's cheap curiosity, so forget it.'

'It's all right. I reminded her of what I'd said at the beginning and I told her it was time to part, that I no longer ... desired her, and when she demanded to know why and what she'd done wrong, I told her that it wasn't her—I'd met another woman I wanted to the exclusion of all others.'

A slight smile flickered about his mouth as their eyes met, and Cadence laughed a little.

'I gather, though, that you didn't tell her who, or

she'd have scratched my eyes out instead of weeping on my shoulder.'

'Yes.' Jon sighed. 'Callous as it sounds, she will get over it. It's the Sashi business I regret more. I didn't know.'

'No. No one told you.' Her fingers tightened on his shoulder and relaxed again.

'You'd have told me. You're not afraid of me, are you, Cadence?'

'No. No, I'm not afraid of you,' she confirmed slowly. 'Just . . . overwhelmed, occasionally.'

'And that's mutual.' His hand was raised to hers where it rested on his shoulder and he lifted it, carrying it to his mouth and brushing the backs of her fingers with his lips. It was in complete contrast to all that had passed between them that morning, gentle and thoughtful, and yet equally compulsive, and it awoke a great rush of tenderness in Cadence. 'Cadence, do you suppose there's any chance of Sashi and Sunila getting back together?'

'That's partly why I was looking for you,' she told him, moving away as he released her hand. 'I believe there is, going by something Sashi said to me, and I'd like to contact him quickly so he can have time to prepare. Do you know where he is, how I can contact him, or do I have to wait for Christo to get back? Or I suppose I could ring our Delhi office for a schedule.'

'I may have the schedule Sunila once gave me somewhere here, if Jahanara hasn't tidied it away,' Jon told her, beginning to search. 'No . . . Wait, here it is. He's actually at Agra today. Here's the number. Do you want to ring now? He could be in. They do the Taj by morning unless there's a good moon. Shall I leave you alone?'

'No, it's all right.'

It took her some time to make contact with Sashi,

however, and while she waited, occasionally reminding the receptionist of her presence on the line while he was being traced, she leaned against the desk and thought about Jon, well aware that he was studying her legs.

The contrast between this morning's storm of passion and this present tenderness was bewildering, especially when the passion had been denied its natural conclusion. And when and where and how had she taken the decision not to berate him for his cruelty to Sunila? She didn't even know what her intention had been as she knocked at the door of this room. Somewhere between her anger over Sunila's hurt and walking in here, something had happened, and she wasn't sure what it was, unless it had occurred to her subconsciously that as cruel as he might be, Jon couldn't be deliberately so, or the Iversons wouldn't love him so much.

Only it was more than that, she thought. This had been her own judgement, her own knowledge of him, not based on outside opinions. Was it something else that she had perceived as they stood staring at each other in that sunbaked courtyard this morning—did it go back that far?

'Yes, I'm still holding on,' she said into the telephone, and smiled at Jon. 'Kipling was right. It's a fool who tries to hustle the East.'

'You've taken to it quickly.'

'The fatal fascination of India,' she laughed.

'It's real.'

Was this also a betrayal of Christopher, this caring and sharing with Jon?

She was put through to Sashi at last, just as the disturbing thought occurred to her.

'Sashi? Cadence Reay. This is a personal call, is that all right? What you were afraid of has happened—Sunila is ... alone and very unhappy and upset.'

'*He Ram!*' Sashi groaned. 'Tell me, Cadence, is she all right? If she is crying, then maybe it is not so bad, but——'

'She has cried a lot,' Cadence reassured him. 'Sashi, when we spoke you implied that if you could have her back——'

'She will not want me, after ... after the other,' he said sadly, and she could picture his disconsolate, dark face.

'I think she might, but she believes you can never forgive her. She's blaming herself very much. That's really all I wanted to say, Sashi, because it's your affair, between the two of you, so it's up to you to handle it as you will. Only I will add this, though you know her better than I, but I think you should give her a while, not too long, then appear and be very masterful. Tell her magnanimously that you forgive her, or be really mean and say you can't forgive her, but are prepared to take her back because you care so much—because she quite genuinely feels just now that she doesn't deserve your forgiveness. Then watch very carefully for the time when she starts feeling she's worn her hair shirt long enough.'

Sashi seemed to ponder this and when he spoke there was a note of amused admiration in his voice: 'I think you may be right, Cadence. You must have been spending a lot of time with her to know her so well.'

'Just today.'

'Then you're a psychologist!'

She looked at Jon when she had said goodbye and replaced the receiver. He was on his feet now and his expression was brooding as he met her eyes.

'The man must hate me.'

'No, he knew you didn't know. It's Sunila who hates you just now, but she'll probably get over it.'

He laughed suddenly. 'And you, Cadence? Why hasn't Aubrey Iverson got you in his Personnel department?'

She shook her head. 'Oh, Jon, for all I know I may have set them on the road to all sorts of misery instead of happiness. I'm sure anyway that they have problems ahead of them. I wouldn't have involved myself at all, except that they involved me by confiding in me, and that somehow gave me a responsibility towards them ... And Sashi does love and understand Sunila.'

'Well, if they ever have cause to be grateful to you, then so will I. It has ... bothered me a bit since you told me about Sashi,' he admitted curtly.

A silence fell and Cadence could feel the atmosphere changing. They were alone together, the problem that had required her to be a friend was behind them, and how could either of them forget for long what lay between them?

With their last turbulent lovemaking so recent, and incomplete, the swift return of tension was inevitable.

Jon asked abruptly, 'Have you spoken to Christopher about Kashmir yet?'

'Yes, but he's not in any hurry to go—you know he doesn't like too much rushing around—and I can't very well explain why we should go.'

'He hasn't guessed?'

'I don't think so.'

'Aren't you sure?'

'I don't know. I keep thinking ... anyone else would have guessed, but Christo is so ... trusting.'

'Especially of us.'

'Oh, Jon, I hate all this,' Cadence confided unhappily. 'We're talking like conspirators ... as if it's us against him, as if I've already been unfaithful to him. I hate it!'

'How do you think I feel?' he grated. 'And don't you think that in a sense you have been unfaithful to him already? Wasn't even the way we were just now a betrayal of his trust?'

'I wondered that too,' she confessed.

There was another tense silence before Jon said, 'We must never be alone together again.'

'I can't bear it!' she exclaimed passionately.

'You must!'

'I want you . . . I want you!' Almost the refrain was an anguished moan as she was swept by a surge of longing and the accompanying tragedy of knowing that it could never be fulfilled.

'Don't say it!' Jon ground out, his face twisting.

But it was too late. The raw pulsating ache of hunger drove them together, and Jon's mouth covered hers with the same savage urgency of that morning, invading, possessing.

Cadence clung to him convulsively, her response frenzied, passionate. The soft sweet melting of initial desire had been a fleeting phase. Now she was rigid, racked with long violent tremors, the need for immediate consummation an unbearable craving, driving her close to insanity.

Jon's mouth left hers to press hot, demanding kisses all over her face, her eyes and temples, the bridge of her nose, her cheeks, her jaw, moving down to her slender neck and the frantic pulse at the base of her throat, while his fingers dug into her, as if he were as out of control as she and unaware of how he was hurting her. Cadence was kissing him back, raining wild kisses all over his face and hair, their mouths colliding, fastening on each other, parting once more to discover new areas.

She could only breathe in long shuddering gasps as she felt his hands at the backs of her thighs, her buttocks, her hips, moving up under her soft coral vest, ceaselessly moving, claiming all of her. Her own fingers scrabbled frantically with his shirt buttons, tearing at them, then tugged insistently at the dark hair covering his damp, heated chest. She felt the spasm that shook him, heard his breath rasp in his throat as his mouth slid to hers again and he gathered her close, holding her so tightly that her hands were trapped between their bodies, kneading at him.

He seemed to surge and thrust against her in some sort of primeval simulation of the act of love, and Cadence arched convulsively, soft sounds of invitation coming from the back of her throat.

'Oh, God, Cadence!' Jon groaned. 'I want you so badly! It gets worse all the time . . . I can't stand it!'

'Jon . . .' She couldn't speak properly, choking on his name as he steered her towards the small couch in one corner of the room.

Entwined, they sank on to it, scattering papers and notebooks, a small cassette-recorder crashing unheeded to the floor. It was only a two-seater couch, small and confining, but they noticed no discomfort, limbs tangled, mouths still devouring. Drawing back a little, Jon thrust up her coral vest to expose the tautness of her unconfined breasts, and bent his dark head to their thrusting temptation.

Shuddering, Cadence gasped as she felt his mouth on the stingingly sensitised flesh, her fingers tightening in his hair as he bathed one swollen, pulsing peak with his tongue. He had one arm about her, holding her, but the other hand continued exploring, stroking up the silken length of her inner thighs that trembled with the need to submit to his maleness.

'Jon!' She cried his name, hands moving to pull him

closer, release him, make their own exploration, draw him back to her once more.

'Why do you do this to me?' he demanded harshly against her breasts. 'How do you? This way! It's never this way with others . . . never this intense. With you, I have no self-control.'

The evidence of his need was rigid against her, and the empty, deprived passage of her womanhood throbbed in response, wanting him, wanting him . . .

'Oh, please—oh, please!' she muttered over and over again, with no control over her maddened senses. 'Jon, I'm going crazy! Oh, please!'

'The door isn't even locked!' Suddenly he was wrenching himself away from her, getting to his feet, but not to lock the door. 'No, Cadence, never again! Did you take in what I said earlier? We must never be alone together again. I will not do this to Christopher and when I'm with you . . . Damn it, I can't help myself, I can't stop myself!'

'Neither can I,' she whispered anguishedly, sitting up and pulling her vest down over her aching breasts, then trying to smooth her hair with trembling fingers. 'Jon?'

'Don't say anything! There's nothing to say.' He stood near the desk now, his back to her. 'Just get out, Cadence, please! Go away—now!'

She stood up, tucking her top back into the waistband of her shorts, and moved towards the door, opening it, knowing he was right. There was nothing to be said, nothing that would help.

She turned to look back at him. He stood with his hands pressed to the desk, leaning over it, head bent and shoulders hunched, as if he were still fighting to gain control of himself.

Jon, she thought regretfully, Jon, my love—I love you.

Being Cadence, she almost went back to tell him, but for once caution swayed her. She left without another word, closing the door and going to her room, her legs starting to tremble violently when she was halfway there.

'I don't believe it,' she muttered furiously as she prepared to wash her hair under the shower, needing action, plenty of action, in order to spend the energy which had been denied its release by Jon's refusal to consummate their passion.

But it was true!

'I just don't understand it,' she said aloud, standing under the shower, noticing faint bruises on her flesh. From this morning or just now? They hadn't been visible when she and Christopher had been swimming.

How could she love Jon Steele when she loved Christopher? And she did love Christopher, she knew that. But she also loved Jon, consumingly, desperately, passionately. She loved him with an intensity that made her want to own him, possess him and never share him with anyone. She would never let him go . . .

How could she love two men? What was the difference? Cadence was invariably honest with herself, but now it was only with considerable reluctance that she acknowledged that her love for Christopher came nowhere near to matching the power and depth of her feeling for Jon. Her love for Christopher was tender, protective . . . motherly?

'Oh, God, what have I done?' she groaned, applying shampoo to her soaking hair.

She loved Christopher the way everyone loved him, because he was so good, but Jon was her man, the man she was designed to love. It was personal, private—and devastating!

She had been so stupid, blithely believing she

controlled her destiny, when all the time this had been waiting for her, this dark possession of the senses, the heart, the soul. All of her belonged to Jon, and had done from that first moment in Bombay, only she had been so accustomed to the concept of herself in love with Christopher that she had failed to recognise it. She had put it down to pure lust, and looked for reasons to hate Jon, stupidly confident that it would pass, when all the time, all that anger she had been feeling was really a distorted manifestation of her love for him. She had gone on believing she would marry Christopher . . .

How could she marry him now, loving Jon like this? Only how could she hurt him either? People didn't hurt Christopher. It was an unwritten rule, obeyed by everyone, even Jon. But to marry him would be to cheat him, and cheat herself too, however happy they might be together. To cheat him . . . or hurt him?

What to do! She just didn't know. Tell Christopher? Tell Jon? Tell no one?

Anyway, Jon didn't love her. He wanted her. Strangely, it didn't seem to matter very much. Cadence understood the proportions of his desire, the extent, the magnitude. His passion for her was out of the ordinary perhaps because, as Christopher had once said, they were so alike, abnormal in their vitality. She knew she could hold Jon for a very long time to come, for years, perhaps even for all their lives. Their passion, once consummated, would not fade and die, but be renewed. It would always flare again. Cadence didn't even bother to question her own certainty. She knew it, in the same unalterable way she knew she loved him.

Only she still didn't know what to do about it, if anything. Her passionate love for Jon was as basic as the earth itself, but the situation was not. Jon and

Christopher, Christopher and Jon ... There was an unusually strong bond between them, and by her love for them both, she too had been bound to them, but somehow the bonds had become an enmeshing tangle, snaring them all, denying them true happiness.

That was the dilemma. If one suffered, they all suffered. There was no solution. Thanks to those bonds, she would no more find pure happiness with Jon than she would with Christopher, and neither could they.

She wanted it all, of course. Like a child, she reflected disgustedly. She wanted Jon, but without hurting Christopher, especially when hurting Christopher meant hurting Jon—and Jon could so easily learn to resent her if in satisfying their mutual need and her love, Christopher became the suffering victim.

Her thoughts went round and round in the same futile circles, and she still had no solution much later when she went down to join the Nayars and Christopher for pre-dinner drinks.

'Jon has asked to be excused,' explained Jaydev.

'He's probably a bit upset about what he had to do. He broke up with Sunila this afternoon and she took it badly,' Christopher offered innocently. 'That's why I had to take her home.'

Cadence looked at him, tenderness and shame mingled in her expression. So much was her fault. She had made the initial mistake, of thinking she loved him in a way that fitted her to be his wife, not just a friend ... He was her best friend still, she realised, but just a friend.

At dinner she ate her vegetable biryani and yoghurt mechanically, her mind still much occupied. Up until now, her life had been miraculously free of dilemma; even small problems had rarely come her way; and now she supposed she was paying for it. But, she thought with a sudden rise of anger, she had always been properly aware of her good fortune and grateful for it, so it was outrageous of Fate to punish her by playing this cruel trick on her.

Her rage died as swiftly as it had risen, as she realised how unreasonable the thought was—and how futile. There was no quarrelling with Fate, no manipulating it. Fate did the twisting, and its victims could only writhe.

Cadence and Christopher occasionally walked to the samand after dinner and they did so tonight, Christopher's arm lying comfortably about her shoulders.

She told him about Sashi Kapur and he said, 'I hope they make it. It's a pity no one had told Jon about him. If he'd known, he probably wouldn't have started anything with Sunila.'

She sighed, thinking—and if he wouldn't have done that to Sashi, he's still less likely to do it to you, his best friend. Except that he wants me more than he can ever have wanted Sunila. How do I know that? I just do.

'What's wrong?' asked Christopher because she had sighed.

Cadence laughed shakily. 'Oh, I was just thinking about the male notion of honour and how from one point of view it can seem rather romantic and admirable, from another, utterly senseless, depending upon who and what is involved.'

She stopped walking, turning and slipping her arms about him, and he held her close, saying whimsically:

'You're in a strange mood tonight, my love. What is it?'

'I don't know.' Her voice was muffled. 'Hold me, Christo.'

'Would you like me to sleep with you tonight?' he questioned her gently.

'I can't, not now,' she whispered.

'Another time, then,' he returned calmly.

Guiltily, she realised he probably thought she had her period. He would make a wonderfully tactful, understanding and considerate husband, but she didn't think she could marry him. Only she didn't think she could tell him either!

'Just hold me,' she said again.

He did, and she felt comfortable and safe and secure because he was her friend. He also kissed her, and all she could feel was a sad tenderness, because there was no magic and no excitement.

Nevertheless, even knowing there was nothing to be recaptured from a past that had been merely an illusion, she tried to respond—because he was Christopher, and because she didn't want to hurt him.

Above them the Indian night sky was a dark silken shimmer, mysterious as the continent it canopied.

Neither of them noticed the tall lean figure striding past some distance away. His eyes were well accustomed to the darkness because he had walked a long way, into the desert and back, but he spared them only a single glance and went on towards the palace.

CHAPTER SEVEN

SHE had to tell them soon, Cadence thought desperately, her hands clenching as her eyes rested hungrily on Jon's dark face.

Jaydev Nayar had turned his polo game into a party. Wives, girl-friends, and other invited guests occupied seats in the shade, a colourful scene with all the vivid saris, gauzy or silk or cotton, and jewellery flashing. Children played on the grass, uniformed servants attended to every need, melting discreetly away afterwards, refreshments were plentiful, and everyone was enjoying themselves.

The chukkas had been spirited and exciting, and Jaydev, Jon, Christopher and one of Jaydev's cousins had emerged as overall winners over Jaydev's younger brother, Hanif Khan, another cousin and a friend from Jaisalmer. Now, with the stable staff having removed the last lot of mounts to be used, the men were standing around as men do after sport, congratulating themselves and each other, with beers—and a soft drink for Hanif, the only Muslim among them and a devastating player, as merciless and daring and yet considerate of his mounts as Jon Steele. They were undoubtedly the stars of the afternoon and responsible for the closeness of the contest.

'Handsome brutes, aren't they?' laughed Padmini, drifting past Cadence and Jahanara where they sat side by side and noticing how their eyes were riveted.

Distracted, the two women looked at each other, and guilty knowledge lay in both pairs of eyes, dark honey and pansy brown. Cadence was aware that an element of constraint had existed between them ever since Jahanara had overheard her and Jon, but she knew there was an additional guilt in Jahanara's discomfort.

The Indian girl, in lilac-swirled trousers and tunic and with her lovely long hair drawn back from her face by two glittering combs, was the first to drop her gaze, her laugh embarrassed.

'They make Hanif look such a boy, and yet he's twenty-six, you know.'

'He's still the handsomest brute of them all, though,' Cadence said fairly, for Hanif was far more conventionally handsome than either Jon or Christopher. 'And when he's wearing one of his natty three-piece business suits, he has an air of maturity.'

'Yes, all serious and responsible.' Jahanara grimaced. 'But at least he isn't as strict with me as our parents were. Cadence . . . do you mind? You don't look well these days. Are you all right?'

Cadence wondered what the reaction would be if she said—I'm dying, I'm dying for want of Jon Steele. That was what it felt like.

But she only said, prosaically, 'I'm a very healthy person, Jahanara. I'm fine, but there has been a bit of . . . stress and strain, as you know. Nothing serious.' Her smile was unusually bitter—she told so many lies these days. 'It's been a lovely afternoon, hasn't it? The Nayars do things with a style that isn't seen too often.'

Jahanara accepted the hint. 'Yes, they manage to retain something of the old days.'

'The good old days, Jahanara?' Cadence raised teasing eyebrows.

'No, mostly bad, I'm afraid.' Jahanara was apologetic. 'It's the harmless, enjoyable aspects these people have retained. These are better days.'

'For all of us.'

'The new freedoms have come sooner to some than to others.' The Indian girl sounded depressed.

'No, Jahanara,' Cadence corrected gently. 'We're all restricted in some way. If not by culture and religion, then by the law, or personal loyalties, personal hangups ... even by love. Love imposes restrictions too, you know.'

Cadence never cried, but there was a stinging and a dazzle in her eyes which had nothing to do with the brilliant Indian sun. The last few days had been unbearable. Unused to lies, even of the silent, loving kind, she knew she could take no more.

Her endurance was at an end. She had to speak, to tell them both, her beloved men. She had to tell Jon—Jon first. It concerned him most, it concerned them both. The decision was theirs to take together, to protect Christopher or to wound him, to deceive or to destroy.

There was no chance that day, however, as all those who had come for the polo stayed on for the party the Nayars gave. It was a lavish affair, the company was charming, and Cadence should have enjoyed it, but Jon was keeping his distance, while she was feeling a fraud, being introduced to people as Christopher's fiancée when she didn't know whether she would have that status for much longer.

Christopher was going to Udaipur the following day, to inspect the hotel there that held the Iverson contract, but Cadence excused herself from accompanying him, guiltily aware that in doing so she aroused no suspicion. The fact that Christopher didn't expect them to do everything together had been one of the aspects of their engagement she had appreciated. They were each free to pursue various activities on their own.

He left the palace in the middle of the morning. Jon

and Jahanara were working, but Cadence knew Jahanara had been given the afternoon off, so she would speak to Jon then, she decided, while she and Padmini were playing with Anjuna in the swimming pool.

As it happened, however, it was Jon who sought her out, shortly before lunch when she had gone to her room to change into one of her newly acquired outfits, this one a simple sundress with a low-cut bodice and back, supported by thin straps tied at the shoulder. The fabric was the usual thin Indian cotton, but of better quality than some she had seen, and the colours of the pattern were dramatic, dark red and brighter red with touches of black and cream, flattering to her deepening suntan.

'Come out,' said Jon when she opened the door in response to his knock.

'Come in,' she retorted, smiling beautifully at him because she loved him so much and didn't have to hide it for the moment.

'No, thanks.' His short laugh contained a hard note. 'I'm not getting caught in your web again. We're less likely to leap on each other out here with the possibility of a servant suddenly appearing and witnessing us.'

Cadence lifted a shoulder and obligingly took one step out into the corridor—a prosaic name for it, because to walk along it was to walk amid gleaming, translucent beauty, for great, ancient marble panels were set at intervals, inlaid with a variety of coloured stones, jasper, cornelian, onyx, turquoise, lapis lazuli and tiger's eye.

'What is it?' she asked.

Jon copied her gesture of a raised shoulder. 'Nothing important as far as I can make out, but since Hanif Khan was so insistent, I promised I'd speak to you.'

'Hanif?'

He laughed sardonically. 'I didn't see much of you at last night's party, but I gather you weren't making too successful a job of hiding your feelings where Christopher was concerned. Guilty conscience, Cadence? Hanif interpreted it differently—as unhappiness, and he imagines he knows the reason. It appears that Jahanara is in love with Christopher. I can't say I'd noticed.'

'I had,' she said quietly.

He sighed. 'I don't think I'm noticing much these days. You don't when you're being rapidly driven crazy ... Anyway, in Hanif's view, it's vitally important that you be reassured that on no account will his sister break up your relationship with Christopher. I tried telling him that I didn't think the possibility could be concerning you, but he insisted that you were so unhappy, you must suspect the possibility. That's the message he wanted conveyed to you, I've performed my task, and the poor man would be shocked to his honourable core if he knew what was really eating you.'

'He meant well and it was sweet of him to be concerned,' Cadence said gently, disliking his cynicism. 'But what would his position be, I wonder, if, say, Christopher also fell in love with Jahanara and I ... I released him? Honour would be an obsession if he objected under those circumstances, but I suppose there would still be other barriers?'

'I'm not sure. He's a very devout Muslim; you've heard the sheer love in his voice when he talks of Allah; but he is also a modern man. He loves his sister and he knows that her commitment to Islam is not as total as his and that he can't force it to be. We've had some long talks about his faith, Hanif and I, and he has actually said this—that he's had to accept that with her absolute femininity, not to mention her love of things that shine and sparkle, Jahanara's major commitment will one day be to a man. So yes, I think that in the end he would yield, reluctantly, but it would have to be marriage or nothing, and he would demand all sorts of assurances and undertakings from the man in question, and especially if he were an infidel. But why make Christopher the man in your hypothesis, Cadence? You know there's absolutely no chance of his ever even looking at another woman.'

'I know. He loves me. But I wish there was the chance, I wish he would fall madly in love with Jahanara!' Her voice had grown stronger and for a moment Jon looked startled.

'Why?' he taunted, eyes glinting with mockery. 'Would it lessen your guilt at lusting after me if Christopher were to stray a little?'

'I don't lust after you!' Cadence claimed tempestuously.

Dark eyebrows rose. 'You could have fooled me.'

'I love you,' she told him passionately.

'What?' There was a momentary blankness, replaced almost instantly by a terrible rage. 'No! No, Cadence, I won't have it! You can't—you mustn't! It's Christopher you love, it has to be. I won't have it!'

He was actually shaking her, lean strong fingers biting into her bare shoulders; shaking her so violently that her upper and lower teeth crashed together and there was a whiteness in her mind.

Between tears and laughter, she gasped, 'You won't have it! Oh, Jon, darling, darling! There's nothing you can do about it, and that's it! I love you! I love you, I love you!'

'No, Cadence, you can't do this! To me, to Christopher!' Jon had stopped shaking her, but his fingers worked agitatedly at her shoulders, his touch enough to make her weak with desire.

'I can't help it,' she told him, warmth and love and distress in her eyes as she lifted her arms to encircle his neck. 'It's true, and I don't know what to do.'

'You haven't told Christopher?' he questioned urgently, his hands dropping to her waist, fingers stretching and spreading over her hips, instinctively drawing her lower body up close against his.

'No, I wanted to tell you first.' Cadence was arching, her pelvis thrust up against his body, and he made a protesting sound.

'You're not to,' he instructed harshly. 'You're not to tell him.'

'I don't want to hurt him, but——'

'Cadence—Cady!' Jon used Christopher's abbreviation for the first time. 'It's not true. In God.'s name, it's not true You've got to love Christopher. I always knew you were dangerous—you'll destroy us all.'

'Do you think I haven't spent days thinking that? I do understand, Jon, but——' She broke off, overwhelmed by the tragic impossibility of their situation and convulsed at the same time by a spasm of pure physical need. 'Kiss me, Jon! Oh, come in and kiss me and love me! Darling . . .'

But it happened right there in the corridor, the first kiss, a violent plundering of her mouth, Jon's need as vast and consuming as her own, obliterating all other considerations.

Then, his breathing fast and uneven, he pushed her back into her room, following and pausing only to slam the door before taking her in his arms again, his mouth crushing hers. Cadence held him and kissed him with a savagery of need that matched his, her hunger ungovernable and still growing.

There was no place for thought. Love and desire

possessed her utterly. She slipped one hand between their stirring bodies, moving downward in compulsive exploration, hearing his hard groan and resenting the barrier of clothing preventing the completeness of knowledge and intimacy.

Somehow they made their way to the low wide bed, with many pauses, unable to stop touching and kissing each other, unable to bear any space between them.

The straps of her dress were already untied as Jon pushed her down on to the soft crimson silk, the bodice fallen down, her breasts free for him to touch and caress, nipples erect, awaiting his further stimulation.

'Jon ... darling, darling!' she gasped ecstatically, looking up into his taut dark face as he moved over her. 'I love you so much.'

'Cadence!' He sounded agonised, as if this were all against his will, but his eyes were glazed and glittering with uncontrollable passion and his hands were at her breasts, massaging, stroking, palpating, a little rough, a little cruel, but she cried out in rapture.

'Kiss me,' she begged huskily, her hands inside his shirt, sliding over his smooth shoulders, worshipping him.

Arms about her now, he pressed his face to her breasts, and she gasped, shaken, at the sweet stab of his tongue against one distended, fiery nipple, darting and flicking, circling and pressing, until she no longer knew if it was pleasure or pain that he inflicted.

She shook beneath him, her passion as wild as his, crying out in rapture as he added sensation to sensation, each one new and different, each a miracle. Sinuous tongue flickered and glided, teeth tugged gently, and pleasure was all that existed in the world, pleasure and wanting, but not yet satisfaction.

'Jon!' Her voice was low and oddly harsh as he

raised his head to look down into her face. She arched against him, writhing and twisting, the rhythm of her hips instinctive and age-old, gyrating, rotating in response to the swollen masculine need commanding her.

His face was agonised, his mouth harsh as it descended to hers once more, and taut rigors shook his long hard body as it lay on hers. His shirt was open now, and the hard, hair-roughened chest that crushed her throbbing breasts was a sweet torture, pain and ecstasy, making her whimper softly.

This time, she thought wildly, it must happen. They couldn't stop this time. She would die——

She hardly recognised her own voice, uttering hoarse throbbing pleas. All the other considerations of days past, all the factors that had held her back, counted for nothing. She didn't even think of them. All that mattered, the most imperative necessity she had ever known, was that she be fully united with the man she loved; to become one with him; an urge that couldn't be denied.

It didn't even matter that he didn't love her. Whatever there was in his feeling for her, his need, it was enough. It might go by the name of desire, or the uglier name of lust, but it was special—exceptional! She didn't need to ask him; she knew he had never wanted anyone—not even his first woman, and how long ago was that?—as intensely, as urgently, as consumingly, as he wanted her.

'Jon, my love, my darling!' The richness of her love, its wealth, made her extravagant in her endearments. 'This time, my dear love, this time? We will, we must . . . Darling, darling!'

'Not this time, sweetheart, not any time.' Jon's voice was rough, as if he were in pain.

Cadence stared at his back as he sat on the edge of

the bed, buttoning his shirt. The greater self-control was his, she realised sadly, because he was not in love.

'Not even after I've told Christopher?'

'You're not going to tell him!' He twisted round to look at her, picking up her left hand, his thumb brushing across her ring. 'You're going to go on wearing this, and you're going to marry Christopher.'

She lay as he had left her, looking up at him. 'How can I? I love you.'

'You love Christopher.' He dropped her hand, but continued to look at her.

'No.'

Cadence felt as if she stood outside of herself, observing the pair of them. It was a phenomenon she had heard and read of, but never previously experienced. What had happened to passion? These two people were so calm, she sad, he serious and intent. He looked at her, saw that her breasts were still uncovered, and pulled the bodice of her dress up over them.

'Sit up and I'll help you,' he said, quite gently.

'No,' she said again, determined to remain where she was. 'I love you and I understand you, Jon, and you want me, in a very special way. We can have a good long time together. How can I marry Christopher, knowing that? How can I cheat him?'

'How can you hurt him?' he retorted, very cold now. 'If you love me, you'll marry Christopher.'

'Now you're trying to cheat me—blackmail me. If I love you, I'll be your woman, I'll live with you, I'll ease whatever this is that's driving you.'

'And the Iversons?' he charged harshly. 'How could I do that to them?'

'I said I understand you, Jon. I understand that you're wrong.' She was trying to speak calmly, but her voice cracked. 'I know these people, remember? They don't expect this of you. They don't expect anything of you. They love you.'

'Just what do you understand?' He was angry now, accusing. 'You know what happened, here in India, when I was a boy. If I hadn't been found, or if I had been found but come under the care of someone other than the Iversons ... Do you understand the disaster my life would have been? Everything I am, all the joy and success that have been in my life since the age of ten ... They're all due to those three people. What they gave me—you've just said it, and you said it too the other day at Amber—what they gave me was love. And how otherwise can I repay them, than by loving them and by not hurting them? Tell me that, Cadence?'

'Love has no price, Jon.' Her eyes flashed with the passion of her conviction. 'It asks for nothing in return.'

'Not even for love?' he taunted. 'You say you love me. Don't you want me to love you?'

'I'd like you to, yes, but I don't expect you to,' she answered clearly.

'Oh God. Why do you have to be so bloody honest?' he asked tiredly.

'Anyway, you do return their love, don't you?' she challenged quickly.

'Yes. They've never needed to hear it, and you don't either. As you say ... you understand!' He was half-serious, half-mocking. 'But what about hurting them, Cadence? Not just Christopher, but Aubrey and Stephanie. They've both written to me about you—they adore you. It wouldn't just be hurting Christopher, but those other two as well.'

There was a silence. They looked at each other, reading truths and lies. Finally, Cadence sat up. Her dress slipped downward again and she hauled it up, dealing with one shoulder strap, but it was Jon who tied the other bow, clumsily but calmly, and it was the hardest thing she had ever done in her life, refraining from flinging herself into his arms.

He said, 'Padmini will be expecting us. Cady? Cadence, thank you for loving me, but . . .' He paused awhile. 'It's Christopher who loves you, so be strong for him—be strong for me! I . . . If I accepted your . . . gift, I couldn't live with myself.'

'You couldn't live with me either,' she stated bleakly as they stood up. She touched his arm. 'That's why I'll try, Jon, my darling Jon, but I can't promise . . . I'm only human, like the rest of you. Mortal!' She paused and the most bitter laugh of her life escaped her. 'If that were all, it might work! But I'm also a woman. What do you know of women, Jon? To us, they're all pointless, these hang-ups . . . nobility and obligation, honour and self-sacrifice, the whole buddy-buddy syndrome. We have strange strengths and weaknesses, we women! Our weakness is our strength, you know. Has that ever struck you? We love men, fools that we are, and that's where our strength lies, in our love . . . Oh, think of it, Jon! Hanif Khan is a better man and loves God or Allah more than you, but he can understand and tolerate our truth, our blasphemy. And you can't.'

He stood looking at her, at the tears in her eyes and the flush of anger in her cheeks.

Finally he said, 'Cady, don't make it so hard on yourself. I'm sorry, God knows, but ultimately you'll be happier loved than loving. Shall we go to lunch?'

They went down together, after she had refreshed her make-up while he stood watching, and they spoke to each other in tight, controlled voices, the words empty and meaningless.

There was nothing left to say, because the situation

was unchanged. Knowing she loved him had not altered Jon's position.

It stayed that way in the days that followed. Cadence suffered as she had never dreamed she could and she was angered by it, because happiness suited her so much better; she was designed and intended to be happy, all that was strong and bright in her resentful of the tragedy that oppressed her. She didn't feel like herself any more, she was a stranger, an anguished, yearning stranger, helpless to settle her own dilemma. That was where so much of the pain lay. The decision had been taken, but by Jon, not by her, and for her own sake as much as for his and Christopher's, she had to abide by it, unaccustomed as she was to being a voiceless and obedient pawn.

It was no consolation to know that Jon too suffered, especially when they couldn't share their anguish and comfort each other. Daily she watched him watching her, and saw her own frustration mirrored in his vivid eyes, saw the tautness of self-control become a harsh, permanent mask. It was sadly ironical; they suffered in the same cause and yet that was what kept them apart—the cause, the unwritten law, which they all obeyed, that the protection of Christopher was paramount. He was to be spared, no matter how deep the anguish to his protectors.

Christopher wouldn't want that, and yet Cadence wasn't sure, had the decision been hers to make, that she wouldn't have chosen as Jon had, even loving him as she did. Nothing would be improved and everything perhaps exacerbated by telling Christopher the truth. At the very least, Jon would resent her for it, or even hate her.

There was no way out, it seemed, no respite from her anguish and frustration, and no cure. Loving Jon was like being caught in an endless violent storm in which all the elements had combined to cause total havoc. She was tossed and pulled by its fury, without relief, wrenched and strained by the intensity of emotions for which there was no outlet, and they were all intense, ranging from passion to concern to a deep tenderness to resentment and back again.

But always, as at the heart of any storm, there was the still, silent centre, and that was the unchanging fact of her love for him and her knowledge of it and its unalterability. That was where the calm and the strength lay.

The violence, the turbulence, she supposed, were because she was in love with Jon; the powerful stillness at their centre was the fact that she loved him. They were different, yet components of the complex whole, just as her physical need of him was part of that whole, making it so complete and so perfect that there could be no questioning, no doubting of the truth. She loved Jon Steele and would always love him.

It showed too, but she guessed that like Hanif Khan, people would make their own interpretations, and only Christopher's was of interest to her.

Ah, dear God, it was cruel, to be so concerned for his happiness that she must watch the man she truly loved suffering for want of her and knowing that he was locked in a similar dilemma, reluctant to wound the family to whom he thought he owed everything and thus forced to watch her suffering, wanting him, when he wanted her . . . a merciless circle.

'I'm thinking of leaving for Kashmir at the beginning of next week,' Christopher announced abruptly one day. 'Cadence, would you mind if I went alone and left you at the palace?'

Cadence stared at him. It was so unexpected that she was speechless. Until that moment they had been talking lightly, laughing at the traffic jam which had held them motionless for twenty minutes already. They had spent the day in Jaipur, just the two of them, and Christopher had visited the City Palace and the famous Jantar Manter observatory while she had inevitably opted for shopping and now owned a vividly dyed bandhani sari, a tiny antique metal scent bottle and a cream skirt and sleeveless jacket adorned with embroidery and the mirror work for which Jaipur was known. They had set out to leave the state capital at what turned out to be its evening peak traffic hour and were now stuck fast in the middle of town, part of a scene of such diversity, colour and humour that Cadence had for a time been partially distracted from her unhappiness.

There were cars, of course, and pedestrians, women in the various styles of Indian dress, men too, though many of the latter wore Western-style clothes, but there were also bicycles, and more small motorcycles than she had ever seen at once before, and camel-carts, the camels standing patiently for all their ill-tempered, unpredictable look, dogs, goats, monkeys, and through all the confusion roamed some of the ubiquitous cows, seeking what they could to devour on the pavements, moving unmolested among traffic and pedestrians and into open-fronted shops, making the statement that here was a Hindu country.

As they looked like being here for some time to come, the most remarkable thing about the chaotic scene was the good nature with which everyone submitted to it. Apart from the camels, every face Cadence could see was quite cheerful, and until Christopher had made his announcement she had been entertained by the smiles and humorous gestures directed at her by two young Indian men on a motorcycle, the one riding pillion looking through an enormous pane of glass which he held across his thighs and which precariously obtruded several feet on either side of him.

'But, Christopher, why?' Cadence stared at him with concern and, had she known it, nervousness in her dark honey eyes, beneath which faint smudges now showed, the result of sleepless frustrated nights.

He looked back at her, almost sympathetically, as if he noted those shadows, the fining of her features, the new vulnerability of the mouth that had once smiled so confidently, and the doubt and anguish in eyes once clear and unafraid.

He said gently, 'You're not very happy, are you, Cadence?'

'Christo . . .' She didn't know how to answer him.

'I know it's not any of the physical ills that so often afflict newcomers to India, I know you love this country already and aren't homesick, I know you haven't had bad news of any of your family or friends at home.' He paused, smiling ruefully. 'So it must be us, our relationship. What's wrong, love, why . . . Sometimes, you know, you actually seem frightened. What is it?'

She was frightened now and incapable of hiding it, her mouth twisting as her slim shaking fingers played nervously with the material of her skirt.

'Christo . . .' As she said his name, so helplessly, a rare bitterness appeared in her eyes.

Her situation had undergone a kind of ironical reverse. Now it was Jon she was in danger of betraying. If she told Christopher the truth, as she was so tempted to do, she would betray Jon, who would not have Christopher told and would not forgive her if she yielded to the temptation.

'You're starting to have doubts, aren't you, my darling?'

'Christopher, I love you!' she exclaimed quickly,

committing herself to the lie—for his sake and for Jon's. 'You know that.'

'But do you love me enough to marry me and not spend the rest of your life wondering if there could have been something more?' he questioned her quietly. 'I love you, Cady, I want to marry you, but only if you're absolutely one hundred per cent convinced that it's also what you want. That's why I think we should have a few days apart. You can think about things, find out if you miss me, that sort of thing.'

'But ...' Cadence shook her head miserably, the guilt revealed by her eyes and flushed cheeks robbing her of speech.

'Who knows?' he laughed kindly. 'You may discover you miss me so much you won't want to spend another minute of your life without me.'

'But Kashmir?' she fell back on a superficial argument. 'You said we'd go together.'

'I'll probably make another trip there before we leave India,' Christopher told her. 'You can accompany me then. Please, Cady, let me do it this way.'

He made so few requests that she knew she would have to yield and ... Oh, God, Jon was going to be furious, and the temptation to the two of them, with Christopher as far away as Kashmir for a few days, so hard to resist.

An idea occurred to her.

'Perhaps it's not such a bad idea, really,' she conceded, unaware that her smile, intended to be bright, was merely brittle. 'You could persuade Jon to go with you ... have some time together without me always around.'

'I don't think he'd come,' Christopher answered. 'Anyway, I ... I feel a need to be alone a while. I'm not sure why.'

She stared at him, compunction pricking as she noticed that he wore a look of fatigue and strain.

'Christo, are you ... Aren't you perhaps the one having doubts?' she asked gently. 'Perhaps knowing that Jon ... your friend ... dislikes me, you've looked at me anew and seen me ... differently?'

Perhaps it would be a solution of a sort, she reflected bleakly, for both men to be free of her—she who had brought about the situation that placed multiple strains on their long friendship. Only, as she had reflected on another occasion, the bonds linking them had been extended to include her too now, and there was no true escape for any of them. Love had never been a liberator; it took captives, imposed restrictions and created inhibitions.

Christopher was laughing at her suggestion, grey eyes with the hint of blue tender and clear and devoid of any sign of dissemblement.

'Ah, never that, Cadence. I love you ... I always will.'

'And I love you,' she murmured, sick with shame, although in a sense it was true, but that was a quibble, a casuistry.

She and Jon between them had cheated Christopher—Christopher who had spoken nothing but the truth.

He would always love her. There was no way out.

CHAPTER EIGHT

CADENCE didn't know whether Christopher had yet informed Jon of his decision to go alone to Kashmir. In the three days since he had told her, she had been reluctant to bring Jon's name up, even in the most casual context, mistrusting her ability to conceal her feelings. It was so difficult to lie, either with words or with silence, and it was even more difficult to look a lie. Unpractised in deception and unable to see her own expression, Cadence could never be sure of whether she concealed or revealed the truth, and the fact that Hanif Khan for one had once registered her unhappiness had unnerved her, even if he had misinterpreted its cause.

So it went on, watching Jon watching her, and wondering if Christopher was watching them both.

But today she could stand it no longer. From a palace window she had watched Jon walk out into the desert as he frequently did, and something seemed to dissolve or give way within her. She followed him.

It was as it had been at Amber, as if finally, her love and desire commanded her utterly. She had no thoughts, not for Christopher who was, in fact, relaxing beside the swimming pool this morning; no thought for anything. She was driven by the demands of her flesh, and her love for the man—the man, the minds, the body. She herself was now mindless, a mass of sheer, trembling need, the need to touch and be touched, to possess and be possessed . . . and ultimately, simply to be with the man she loved.

Unlike that morning at Amber, however, Jon was

unaware of her following him. He had a long stride, but with a little effort Cadence was closing the gap between them. Heedless of the dusty scrub and the sweltering heat of the blazing day that raised a film of perspiration on her skin and made her pale olive-green top cling damply to her, she followed a shimmering vision, of a tall dark man in jeans and thin cream shirt, which filled her entire consciousness, sight and mind and heart, to the exclusion of all else.

Finally, she must have made some sound that reached him, because he stopped and turned. Cadence went on walking, though, and they stared at each other through the oiled, rippling effect of the waves of heat that rose from the desert floor.

Then Jon stirred and began to walk back towards her. Neither of them spoke. It was as it had been at Amber. He knew why she was here and they both knew what was going to happen. It was something they both needed.

Feet in the dust, and the scorching desert heat about them, they stood locked together once again, frantic mouths devouring, febrile hands grasping and exploring. Above them the Indian sun was a ball of white fire, almost too big for the burnished sky, filling and blanching it with its dazzling light.

It was a world of heat. The filigreed palace with its cool marbled interior, its lotus pools and fountains, was not far behind them, but it seemed to recede, a shimmering dream picture, like a mirage, with no reality in this arid, sunbaked world.

A world of heat, but Cadence and Jon were conscious only of the personal, intimate heat their wild passion generated, the swirling interior heat of a savage desire that must be sated or topple them into madness, and the heat of their stirring bodies. They were both wet with sweat, their clothes clinging to them, but the discomfort counted for nothing beside their need to be in each other's arms, mouths searingly merged, loins leaping and quivering with the agonies of desire.

Jon groaned agonisedly and Cadence felt him shudder tautly against her, knowing that for him too those first transitory moments of relief and almost-joy as they fell into each other's arms had passed. Now there was only a bitter frustration as they strained frenziedly for a greater closeness, trembling and swaying under the force of their hunger, arms aching as they clung convulsively to each other.

'Jon ... Jon, darling!' His name emerged as a feverish, breathless mutter as he raised his head to look down into her flushed face.

Cadence stared at him desperately, willing his compliance, praying for it, in no doubt that his hunger was as vast and engulfing as hers. He was pale beneath his tan, his face perspiration-beaded, his eyes brilliant and bitter with a savage need, glittering down at her, more blazingly blue than she had ever seen them, and against her breast she felt the crazy thudding of his heart, racing and pounding like her own.

With another anguished groan, a strangled sound as if he were losing the battle for mastery, Jon dropped his mouth to the pulsing, rosy temptation of hers. His hands were at her hips, drawing her up against him, and Cadence writhed, twisting and turning about him, feeling the hard, throbbing potency of his need.

There was nothing of gentleness in their embrace. Mouths were savage, hands urgent, bodies rigid, shaken by spasms of desire. If this was sensuality, it was of the fiercest, most basic kind, their need far beyond the merely erotic. It was a simple, fundamental necessity, as vital and undeniable as their need for air and water and food. The time for tenderness would not be until that primary requirement was fulfilled and they were mated, their phenomenal sexual energy spent for a time.

Soft savage little sounds came from Cadence's throat. She wanted him, here and now, in the burning dust at their feet. She was consumed by her need for his possession, for total knowledge of him, her wanting like a dark, pulsating wound that cried out for assuagement.

But Jon was thrusting her away from him and taking a step backward.

'No!'

'Jon!' It was a wild, agonised cry of pain and she felt their sudden separation like an amputation, as if sundered from some vital part of herself.

Breathing hard, he stood looking at her for a few moments, a dark violence in his face as he surveyed the tautly quivering lines of her aroused body, the wetly clinging upper garment, and the suffering shape of her swollen, inflamed mouth. Above her anguished face, the honey-gold streaks in her fringe were darkened as it lay in damp strands across her brow, and her eyes too were darkened, a bitter light of deprivation in their depths.

For a moment he looked away, past her, towards the dream palace, a blurred fantasy of grace and fairytale beauty, its solid, majestic reality softened, veiled by the distorting heat haze. Then he looked at Cadence again.

'It doesn't help, don't you see?' he challenged savagely. 'I know why you're out here, but it doesn't help, to be like this ... to start this, when we can't finish it.'

'And why can't we finish it?' she flared, as savage as he. 'Because of some stupid masculine ethic—some silly schoolboy code of honour!'

It was unfair and she knew it, but the empty, crying space inside her which he should have filled was an actual ache. She felt hollow, bereft, and she could not contain her resentment. He had denied her her most basic function as a woman, because men and women had different values, different priorities. They always had had and probably always would have. It was the way of humankind, and Cadence wondered angrily at the uneven design which had created such incompatibility between two sexes who yet couldn't live without each other.

'I thought you had understood,' Jon said flatly.

The rage went out of her and her shoulders slumped. 'I do,' she conceded shakily. 'I'm sorry. But I'm a woman, I reason differently——'

'If you reason at all,' he inserted satirically.

'And I love you!' Cadence's voice rose.

Jon flinched. 'Stop telling me that!'

'Why should I?' A bitterly mocking laugh escaped her. 'That's one thing you can't stop or alter, Jon. My love is mine, to give where I will, even where it's not wanted. I love you, I will always love you, I will die loving you.'

'You love Christopher!' Jon was on the verge of losing his temper.

'In another way altogether, the wrong way for lovers,' she said sadly. 'Incidentally, has he told you yet?'

Jon's eyes grew wary. 'Told me what?'

'That he wants to go to Kashmir alone. He's leaving me here with you, Jon,' she taunted. 'He's leaving me here to . . . to Think Things Over.'

'You bitch! What have you been saying to him? What did you tell him?'

'Nothing,' Cadence snapped. 'But unfortunately, I happen to be a bad actress. He's noticed or sensed, I don't know which, that I . . . that I'm dissatisfied, and he thinks I may be having second thoughts about our engagement.'

'Does he——' Jon stopped abruptly.

'Does he suspect? Does he guess?' she supplied more gently. 'I don't know, Jon. He hasn't said anything, and you'd think he would if he did . . . suspect the truth.'

'Not everybody says everything straight out the way you do, Cadence,' Jon stated tautly.

'And anyway, as I've just been saying, men are different.' She laughed hollowly at the obviousness of that. 'So different I'm beginning to realise that, much as he loves me, Christopher would probably sit down and discuss it with you first if he did suspect.'

'Well, he hasn't done so.' Jon didn't question her supposition.

'There you are, then.'

His mouth twisted. 'It means nothing. You ought to know. Christopher never rushes in. He has a reflective nature and likes to be sure of his facts before acting. Cadence, I know it's hard for you, that you're not used to dissembling, but you've got to make a real effort to persuade him that everything is perfect in your relationship, that you're entirely satisfied . . . You've got to make him take you to Kashmir with him.'

'I did try,' she told him. 'And I also suggested that the two of you go off and leave me, but . . . he wants to be alone, Jon.'

'Oh, God,' he said resignedly. 'I couldn't have gone anyway. I've had enough time off and I'm supposed to be working. But even that's no longer coming easily. Jahanara thinks I've gone crazy, and she's right.'

Cadence looked at him, and her heart seemed to swell with love for him. Frustration had stamped his face with cruel savagery, she saw. The sockets containing the vivid eyes were darkly shadowed and his mouth was a grim line.

'Jon,' she ventured quietly. 'Darling? Can't we tell Christopher the truth? I can't go on much longer like this. Can you?'

'We have to,' he asserted emphatically, eyes blazing. 'We have to go on. I've explained to you about the Iversons, and you know as well as I do how hurt they would be. I owe them too much.'

'Jon, how can you be so blind?' Cadence asked, and tears of frustration stood in her eyes. 'They love you. They wouldn't want you to suffer . . .'

'Granted, but they sure as hell wouldn't expect me to gratify my physical desires at Christopher's expense!' he exploded.

Of course, she thought sadly. She had forgotten he didn't love her—a strange thing to forget, and stranger still that it had never seemed to matter very much. He only wanted her.

'Jon, for pity's sake,' she tried again. 'We're all adult men and women, you and I and Christopher, Stephanie and Aubrey. We're not saints, not even Christo; we're ordinary, quirky, subjective human beings. We can't love, or want, to order, and I'm sure we all accept that. Life and love aren't some sort of puzzle where all the pieces fit perfectly. The Iversons are realists, they know that! Like the rest of us, they expect to have to suffer at some stage of their lives, to lose out, and I believe they're strong enough, and mature enough, and sensitive enough, to handle it. Christopher as well as his parents. You don't seem to have much respect for them.'

'For God's sake, Cadence, don't you think I know all that you're saying about them is true?' Jon demanded tiredly. 'I've known them for twenty-five years, remember. But I also know what I would be today, if it wasn't for those three people. I know what I was well on the way to becoming, when they took me into their home.'

'All right, I understand that and I'll try to accept it.' Cadence was endeavouring to speak calmly, although all her inclination was to weep or rage. 'But what about me, Jon? I love and admire the Iversons, but I don't owe them your sort of debt. I wronged Christopher by thinking I loved him enough to marry, and I'll be compounding that wrong if I don't admit it to him. This is why people have engagements instead of marrying immediately——'

'You'd be married by now if I'd agreed to go home before next April,' he reminded her. 'Listen to me, Cadence. There's absolutely no point in your breaking your engagement. I'll never touch you again if you do. I'll never touch you again anyway, God give me strength!'

She sighed. 'Jon, there's a side to this, a point of view, that has nothing to do with you, or even with Christopher. It's to do with me. Even if you didn't . . . want me like this, if you'd never looked at me, if it all came from my side with absolutely no reciprocation . . . Even then, how could I marry Christo? Apart from cheating him, I'd be cheating myself. Live your lies of silence, I do understand your need, but I have to be true to myself. I won't mention you.'

'Damn you,' he said wearily. 'I'd still know it was because of me, even if they didn't. How do you think I'd feel, knowing I was responsible for their . . . disappointment?'

'You're not responsible—I am. I love you. That's me. You had nothing to do with it.'

'I existed,' he retorted unanswerably. 'And I fed it. Cady, Christopher loves you.'

'I know,' she breathed regretfully. 'I wish I loved him . . . for all our sakes . . . but it's you, Jon.'

'How much do you love me?' he asked oddly.

A deep, warm glow was growing in her eyes as she considered the strange question.

Finally she said, 'Do you remember when we talked about *sati*, Jon? I thought it was horrible, but I can understand it now . . . That's how much I love you. I suppose I can live without your love, without you, here in the world, because I'd still be sharing something with you . . . life, the world. But if you weren't here, if you were dead, then I . . . couldn't. I understand *sati* now.'

Jon's face was an expressionless mask. 'That's a lot of loving, Cadence . . .'

She smiled faintly. 'So take care of yourself, my darling.'

'You burden me with the need to do so,' he retorted sardonically.

'I'm sorry, but you asked. I told you.'

'Cadence, if you love me so much . . .' He had begun slowly, steadily, but now, oddly, he hesitated. 'You'll marry Christopher.'

The glow had gone from her eyes, but the love remained, and a sad acceptance.

'For you? Because you ask it?' Her voice sounded small and stifled.

'Yes, I know it's blackmail and I'm not proud of myself, abusing your . . . Oh God, Cadence!' he exclaimed disgustedly, and she heard some of her own despair there. 'You see——'

'It's all right, Jon,' she interrupted gently. 'I know . . . I understand what it means to you.'

'Cadence——' He stopped abruptly, as if he simply didn't know how to continue.

'It's all right,' she said again. 'I'm no good at hiding

things, but ... I'll try, Jon. I'm going back to the palace now. It's crazy to be standing here in this heat. Are you coming?'

He inclined his head and fell into step beside her.

'I know it's grossly unfair to you,' he said quietly after a minute. 'Asking you to live a lie when it's so alien to your nature, and to cheat yourself——'

'That's how much I love you.' She shrugged resignedly, her face pale.

'But it won't be cheating Christopher.'

'It really is for his sake, isn't it?' she realised slowly, glancing at him. 'It's nothing to do with your conscience or honour or anything, it's just for him.'

'I have to give them something back.'

'Christopher wouldn't accept it if he knew.'

'But he won't know. Will he?'

'No,' Cadence sighed the word, a tiny sound, and went on walking, keeping her eyes focused on the palace ahead.

It had to be faced. Of course, she had always known it, without ever really thinking about it, that great disparity which made him choose her rather than Christopher to be the suffering victim of this intolerable situation. He cared about the Iversons—he merely desired her.

As they approached the palace and the moment of their parting, Jon said, quite gently, 'At least Christopher loves you, Cadence.'

'And you don't.' She saw the dark head move in acknowledgement and wondered why this particular truth didn't hurt more. 'Who are you trying to reassure, Jon? Me, or yourself?'

He swore bitterly, in protest and despair, and she realised he must be as unhappy as she was. A change had taken place, as it had after he had ended his relationship with Sunila de Souza. They had been talking on an emotional level and so she could touch his hand now in a gesture of both contrition and comfort without the intrusion of the sexual feeling that normally flared at any contact between them.

'Never mind,' she said inadequately, trying to sound philosophical, but her voice broke a little. 'We won't talk about it any more. I never realised how much hotter it was out here, just a tiny way out into the desert . . . Padmini says a nuclear device was exploded in the Rajasthan desert in the seventies.'

'Cadence, don't!' He had detected the brittle, forced note, the desperation, almost, with which she strove to keep talking.

'It's funny, really.' There was an edge of hysteria to her laughter. 'We're a bit like nuclear powers, Jon, aren't we? Whoever we choose to destroy, Christopher or each other, we're running the risk of our own destruction too!'

'For God's sake! Cady, I'm sorry!' he said violently, bitterly, and this time it was he who touched her hand. 'There's no alternative.'

'I know,' she sighed, controlling herself. 'And I will try, Jon, I promise you.'

For his sake, because she loved him.

She did try. She began by trying to persuade Christopher to take her to Kashmir with him. She even told an outright lie, claiming that she loved him and was still as ecstatic as ever about their engagement, but being Cadence, she told the lie badly, and she nearly wept to see him look so disappointed in her.

'Happy, Cadence?' he teased with gentle reproach. 'Look in a mirror, my darling.'

Next she considered telling him that frustration was her trouble, but if by some miracle he believed her and offered to relieve it, the lie would still be discovered,

because how could she respond to him, wanting Jon as
she did? Perhaps if and when she married Christopher,
as Jon insisted she must, she would somehow find the
strength or talent to simulate response, but not now,
not with Jon so near . . .

When the time came for Christopher to leave for
Kashmir, Cadence clung to him, almost tearfully, and
so afraid, desperately afraid, that this might be the last
time she could do so with even a vestige of what
passed for innocence, distrusting both her own
strength of will and Jon's.

Whatever reason he had given Jaydev and Padmini
for his decision to go to Kashmir alone, they seemed to
have accepted it and showed no puzzlement that
Cadence noticed. On the other hand, no one had
thought to mention the arrangement to Jahanara
Khan. She was shocked to find Christopher gone and
Cadence still at the palace, and was initially inclined to
think it was Cadence's doing.

'How can you let him go on his own, Cadence?' she
asked worriedly when she heard. 'Your fiancé? You
ought to be together.'

'I know, but he wanted to be alone,' Cadence
vouchsafed with some reserve, unsure how much she
ought to confide in Jahanara—poor Jahanara who was
hopelessly in love with Christopher.

Jahanara's eyes widened. 'He chose to go alone?'

'Yes, and not all my arguments and pleading could
make him change his mind,' Cadence said lightly, but
her expression was sad and serious.

So was Jahanara's, her dark eyes grave and
troubled. 'But why? I don't understand it! He . . . he's
driving you into Jon's arms.'

Cadence was also afraid of that, but she didn't say
so. What lay between Jon Steele and herself was far
too personal and painful to be referred to.

She felt desperately sorry for Jahanara, but they both hid or tried to hide guilty secrets, which inhibited them, preventing complete candour. They had both broken the rules, she by loving Jon, Jahanara by loving Christopher. Cadence had no doubt that Jahanara's love for Christopher was real and deep, not just a product of her romantic nature and admiration for his fair looks. For one thing, it was a generous love that put Christopher's happiness first; if he could only find happiness with Cadence, then that was what Jahanara wanted for him, but if he could have found it with her, then the gentle Jahanara would have defied both her brother and the most powerful faith on earth to give it to him.

If only ... Sadly, Cadence put the wish away. There was no hope that way. Without conceit, she knew she was the only woman Christopher would ever truly love.

To be loved was nice; it was warming; and Christopher would have been appalled had he known of the agony his enduring love was causing her.

It was becoming intolerable. Deeply ashamed, Cadence realised that in his absence, the temptation to be unfaithful was stronger than ever before, and she knew that Jon was experiencing the same thing. She didn't need to be told. She saw him daily, and she understood, reading his frustration, his hunger, and seeing the cracks that began to appear in his self-control. She knew so many of his moods now, and the darkly brooding, the irritable, the sardonically taunting, all signalled the war he was waging with himself—and losing? She was losing hers.

Guiltily, she wondered if it was actually Christopher's absence that made the temptation so much greater. It would be easier to cheat and not be found out ... Were she and Jon that selfish, or did their reasons for concealment acquire them a little merit? The real answer was very simple, she suspected. They were man and woman, ordinary fallible mortals, just like the rest of the human race, with more potential to be sinners than saints. They had assumed a burden too big for their mortality and they were even greater fools if they expected to withstand the strain.

Probably Christopher's absence had nothing to do with the increase of temptation. Quite simply, she and Jon were reaching breaking point.

Always at this stage in her thoughts, Cadence would experience a wave of self-disgust. She was attempting to justify in advance their betrayal of Christopher— but it would not happen, it must not! They wouldn't let it!

But there were hours when it seemed inevitable. Their control was made of such frail fabric, and was already rent and tattered from all the other times they had faced temptation and yielded without ever yielding completely, whereas their need for each other was such a vast and powerful thing, dominating them both, and how could they deny it?

At times it seemed to her as if the responsibility to be strong lay with Jon alone. He ought to be the stronger, she thought almost resentfully, because he loved the Iversons and he didn't love her; but it was always her mind talking. Somewhere else, in the places where she loved him, those dark recesses that went by the name of the heart, and where instinct reigned supreme, she knew that they shared the responsibility equally. If he would be strong for Christopher's sake, then she must be strong for Jon's.

If they weakened and failed, they would both be to blame . . . But who would blame them? The Iversons, and Christopher especially, would be hurt, but they would make no accusations; they would not judge and condemn them.

But Jon would point a finger, at himself, and at her, and Cadence knew she could not bear that. Self-hatred was the most blackly miserable emotion in the world, and if she helped Jon to that, then she too would be its prey because she could never forgive herself.

Jon kept to the palace, working, driving himself and Jahanara hard, so Cadence took to going out as often as possible, making constant use not only of one of Jaydev's cars, but a driver as well, since the consequences of acccidentally running down one of Hind's sacred wandering cows didn't bear contemplation. She was still finding things to buy, so she went shopping frequently, alone or with Padmini and occasionally with Jahanara when Jon gave her time off.

She also visited the Khans in their home again and was impressed anew by Hanif's courtesy and charm, as well as by the way he explained Islam to her. It was a welcoming religion, and she suspected he wouldn't have been averse to trying to convert her when he realised her respect and interest, but devout as he was, he was a moderate rather than a fanatic, and he was too polite and reserved to press it.

Another outing she arranged was to meet Sunila de Souza, and she learned that Sashi Kapur had been in touch with her and that Sunila was just beginning to dare to hope that things might one day be as they were between them before the advent of Jon Steele in her life.

Cadence longed to report this to Jon, but she had reached a state where even in the restraining presence of Jaydev and Padmini she could not address him directly without revealing her feelings.

She had accepted an invitation to go with the Khans to Fatehpur Sikri, the red city built in honour of the birth of Emperor Akbar's son, a day trip, and was dismayed when she learnt that Jon was accompanying them.

'I'm sorry,' he murmured in reply to her questioning look later as they strolled among the red stone buildings in the most intense heat Cadence had so far experienced in India. 'This is one of Hanif's favourite places and I had promised to accompany them a long time ago. I didn't know they would be inviting you, although I should have thought of it.'

'Jon . . .' Her voice was yearning and she swayed a little towards him.

'Oh, God, I wish Christopher would come back!' he exclaimed with savage despair.

'I thought that too at first, but it's not because Christopher is away,' she said softly. 'I think it would be exactly the same if he were here.'

'I know. It's got beyond . . . controlling.' Jon sighed and then added violently, 'Help me, Cadence!'

'I'm trying,' she whispered helplessly. 'But Jon, I'm only human, the same as you.'

'You're strong!' It was almost a plea.

'I've told you where a woman spends her strength. In loving—and loving you makes me weak.'

She turned from him then, aware of Jahanara waiting for them to catch up, her dark eyes suspicious and sad, and Cadence knew her anxiety was for Christopher and well justified.

A sigh shook her. They all loved the wrong people, she and Jahanara and Christopher, while Jon didn't love at all in that way, though he suffered as cruelly as she, and there was no hope for any of them. Love was the least ordered of things in a disordered world, wayward, capricious and wilful.

So it was pointless to rebel, although all her instincts urged rebellion. To have no choice and no say was perhaps the greatest frustration of all, but how could she try her hand at ordering things differently when she couldn't even dictate to her own heart?

These thoughts were still with her late that night, back at the palace, as she lay sleepless in her sumptuous room, restless and unhappy, the ache in her heart and the hunger in her loins intolerable.

She had bathed and gone to bed at eleven, risen angrily again just before midnight and roamed about doing little things like practising donning and walking in the saris she had purchased, giving herself a manicure and pedicure, writing to her family and friends. At one-thirty, she had turned out the lights and tried again, but half an hour later she knew it was hopeless.

Still she lay there, alternating between despair and anger, while all the time her heart and her body called to Jon, with such an intensity of longing that it was almost as if they willed him, and surely he must hear their call and come.

But he didn't.

Did he sleep, she wondered, or did he lie awake like her, or was he down in that study he used, working?

Almost, she rose up to go and find him, but she knew he would never forgive her. To go to him in these still, dark hours, when the soul was at its loneliest, could have only one outcome.

The moon shone now, casting a strange, beautiful pattern on the pale marble floor and rich carpets as it streamed through the stone-filigreed window. All the world outside would be washed in its soft, bright mother-of-pearl radiance.

Without putting on the light, Cadence got out of bed again and went to look out. Her room overlooked the inner garden, and the lotus pool caught her eye first, its water a silver shimmer, its burden of flowers closed and blanched to ghostly white.

Then she saw Jon. He stood by an ornamental wall to one side of the lotus pool, so still that she could almost feel the pain of his rigid tension.

That was when the last fragile remnants of her strength and control fell away from her.

Not that Cadence thought of it that way now. She wasn't thinking. That mindless compulsion, almost a trance, which had possessed her at Amber and in the desert, drove her now. Jon was calling to her, and she was answering.

Automatically, she put on her robe before slipping out of her room and making her way along the softly lit marbled corridor to the broad, graciously curving flight of stairs at the end. No fears or inhibitions troubled her now, nor even Jon's own wishes in the matter. He wanted her, and her blood ruled her utterly, responding to the summons of his. This wasn't a matter where the mind or conscience played any part. She was governed solely by the heart and the flesh.

The velvet warmth of the Indian night enveloped her as she let herself out of the cool air-conditioned palace by one of the many exits and went towards Jon. He turned, long before she reached him, and registered no surprise. He knew as surely as she, as he began to walk towards her. There would be no protest and no denial.

His arms were open and Cadence walked straight into them, shaken by a long shivering sigh as they folded round her and she understood for certain that he had given up the struggle.

Briefly Jon raised his face to the sky, eyes closed, a gesture that could have been relief or despair, prayer or praisegiving.

'I can't any more, Cadence,' he whispered. 'I have to, I must . . . I can't fight it any longer.'

CHAPTER NINE

'CAN I make you pregnant?'

'No. I take the pill.'

It couldn't have made any difference had Cadence's answer been otherwise. What was going to happen was inevitable, and she and Jon both knew it. It was this sure knowledge that had enabled them to walk calmly together to Cadence's room, hand in hand, but without touching in any other way; and it was this knowledge that had touched their preliminary love-making with an indescribable pleasure.

Always before, in each other's arms, there had been an anguish, a frustration, because at the back of their minds had lain the knowledge that they must stop, that there would be no full coming together.

But not tonight. The urgency, the need, the hunger were still there, but none of the agony. All past considerations and conflict had been obliterated by the passion that had been growing and growing between them in the days and weeks gone by until now at last it was become so vast, so overwhelming, that there was no room for anything else.

Intellect had no place here, and it was no deliberate decision they had taken. They were merely obeying a compulsion too powerful to be resisted, and they revelled extravagantly in yielding to its domination at last, as if all the self-denial of other occasions had earned them the right to be together finally.

The covers of Cadence's bed were thrown back as they lay together, both naked now, in the soft golden light of the single lamp they had paused to switch on, and the vast torrent of passion that had been unleashed with their first kiss gathered in strength and intensity, sweeping them along, commanding them utterly.

Desire had conquered them and in doing so freed them. They responded to each other with a tempestuous lack of restraint. They spent themselves lavishly, generous in pleasuring each other, prodigal of their kisses and caresses.

A rage of love and longing, violent and uncontrollable, had shaken Cadence when she saw Jon's unclothed body for the first time and felt his nakedness against hers, his strength and hardness, the throbbing potency of his hunger, promising her rapture. She had possessed him with her hands and mouth, every inch of him, utterly confident as she attended to his pleasure as passionately as he did to hers.

Still his hands and mouth explored her polished skin, intimately and hotly, and she writhed and twisted erotically against him, seduced to mindless pleasure and half-crazed with anticipation. Her breasts were tumescent beneath his mouth, the nipples engorged, sensitised almost beyond endurance by his tongue and teeth, pleasure so exquisite it was nearly pain.

'Jon! Darling, darling Jon!' Cadence could only gasp the endearments, her head thrashing from side to side against the pillows now, as his mouth travelled the passage of pleasure his hands had already created. He was kissing her feet, her ankles, her inner knee, tongue applying spirals of sensual delight to the searing flesh of her trembling thighs, moving upward until she cried out in an excess of ungovernable rapture and wanting.

A wild gratitude made her stir violently, drawing

him up to her again, so that once more she might
adore him with her mouth and hands, beginning at his
own mouth and throat, moving to his shoulders and
down, fingers and tongue caressing the sharp stab of
male nipples and moving on again to the flat stomach
and the tautness of his thighs, revelling in his male
beauty, his pulsing virility, worshipping, until he
made a sharp protesting sound and pushed her back.

Jon moved over her, his springy body hair strangely
soft yet harsh against her skin, and Cadence arched,
moaning, as impatient now of these preliminaries as
he. Her need of him was a hot pulsating ache, and she
looked up into his dark face, finding in it an almost
savage intensity, his mouth compressed, his eyes
feverishly glittering.

'Jon . . . Darling, I love you, I love you!'

She held him tightly, parting her thighs for him,
opening to him. For timeless moments they clung
convulsively to each other, desire-congested bodies
wet and slippery with perspiration, and racked with a
passion that was imperative, urgent and elemental.

'Cadence!'

She felt him surge and rear against her, then gather
himself in the last moment of control that was left to
him, and her body leapt to welcome the invasive thrust
of his.

It was basic and utterly necessary, so much wanted
and so long denied that it was inevitably a swift and
savage union. They moved together strongly, perfectly
matched, and Cadence's cries of love rang through the
room. Rapidly, as one, they reached a shattering,
uninhibited climax, and she held Jon within her in a
paroxysm of purest rapture as they shared the rare
dark ecstasy that set and sealed for ever their mutual
dependence, truly one at last, bodily and spiritually
it seemed to Cadence, as if this were the fate that had

been written for them at the beginning of time. In that final moment, the little death, the darkness passed; her mind was expanded, filled with a clear light, and she saw and understood all things that were of herself and Jon, and knew that this could not be either an end or a beginning because destiny was an ongoing and infinite adventure.

Divinity, she thought as she sank into warmth and a wondrous lassitude. That was what had been granted to them in those moments, the small escape from mortality and the world that made the difference between humans and animals. Eyes shut, she smiled against Jon's shoulder as her breathing grew slow and low, barely perceptible. She still felt like a goddess; anything was possible and nothing had any limits; she would never let him go, and he could never let her go. They belonged . . .

A whisper of a laugh escaped her. These were such big thoughts, grandiose really, and yet they seemed entirely reasonable and justified.

Then she stopped thinking and lay quietly, simply feeling, loving Jon, one hand resting against his side, and warmth and a honeyed tenderness seemed to envelop them both.

After a while Jon sighed and stirred, and Cadence clung to him, making soft little sounds of love and protest because he seemed to want to move away from her.

'Cadence?'

She opened her eyes as he shifted again. He had raised himself on one elbow and lay on his side, looking down into her face, studying her with an expression she couldn't properly identify because it seemed to combine regret and tenderness with a few other emotions.

'Jon.' She lifted her arms to encircle his neck, smiling radiantly, overwhelmed by an excess of love.

'Jon, my darling, my love . . . my prince! That's why you're here in this place, Rajasthan, the abode of princes. You're a prince among men!'

He laughed a little shakily. 'You're so very extravagant, sweetheart. I'm not even thinking very much of myself as a man at this moment.'

Catching the note of strain, she released him with a sigh, a little of her euphoria receding as she faced reality once more, and knew the grandeur of her earlier thoughts for a delusion.

Sitting up, Jon reached for the upper sheet and pulled it up over her. Then he looked at her again.

'I didn't know, I hadn't realised that Christopher had never been your lover.' He seemed to be choosing his words very carefully. 'Nor did I . . . guess that you had never had any lover.'

'I thought he might have mentioned it to you.'

'No, we haven't gone in for that sort of discussion,' Jon told her drily. 'Plus, I've done my best to discourage him from talking about you at all. But why are you . . . using contraceptives, then?'

It was her first moment of shame. 'I had thought it . . . might happen while we were in India and I wanted to be prepared,' she confessed with a touch of sadness, knowing what she was doing to him.

'Why didn't it . . . happen?' he asked stiltedly.

'By the time he asked me, I knew I was in love with you,' she explained quietly.

'Oh, God.' His voice was flat and lifeless as he turned his back on her.

'Jon.' She lifted a hand, laying it along his spine, but there was no response.

'So I've not only stolen this time from him,' he continued after a while, still in that dead, despairing voice. 'I've had . . . what he hasn't. I've stolen what should have been your gift to him.'

'I gave it to you, darling.'

'You squandered it, I took it.'

'Do you blame me?' she asked unhappily.

He looked at her then, his face dark and bitter. 'How can I blame you any more than I blame myself? We were both equally involved, we were both here.'

'You asked me to help you, you wanted me to be strong . . . for you, because I love you,' she reflected regretfully. 'And I failed you.'

'We both failed Christopher,' Jon corrected harshly.

'When I saw you out there . . .' Her voice trailed away. 'I can't explain it, Jon, but I had to . . . I had to!'

'I know,' he sighed. 'If you hadn't come to me, I think I might have gone to you . . . I couldn't take any more.'

'Have I . . . have I made you hate yourself?' Cadence's voice cracked a little.

'I hate myself, but don't burden yourself with that, Cadence,' he advised unsteadily. 'Don't you have your own load to bear? Don't you hate yourself a little? Don't you feel guilty as hell?'

'Only a little,' she pronounced candidly, sitting up and putting her arms round him, pressing her breasts against him. 'Not as much as you, my darling. I just wish I'd told Christopher before . . . Then there would be no shame—for me. It's different for me, isn't it? I feel I had a certain right . . . because I love you.'

The look he gave her was oddly blank, and she sighed, realising he was not yet to be won. She was losing him again.

To underline that fact, he said, 'You do understand, Cadence? That this is all, that it can't happen again? This is all there can be.'

'And I'm to carry on as before, and Christopher is

to remain in ignorance?' she challenged with a bitter anger.

'Cadence...' His breath seemed to catch in his throat and he stopped.

'Deceiving Christopher, letting him live in a fool's paradise!' she lashed. 'Isn't that greater cause for shame than what we've done here tonight, Jon?'

'Cady. Oh, God, I can't take what's his ... not another time,' he protested achingly.

'You're twisted—warped!' she accused brokenly.

'Cadence, please! Don't cry,' he whispered, his arms about her as she shook, but her sobbing was dry, her anguish too great for tears, incapable anyway of being eased by the relief they would have brought.

'This is all I'm to have?' she choked.

'I'm sorry, but yes!' Jon sounded as distressed as she, but resolute.

'This night?' she questioned him with sudden violence.

'Cady——'

'This night, Jon, this whole night? You can't leave me now! You can't leave me tonight!'

And it was true. Their energy was flaring anew, sexual tension quivering between them once more, and she felt him already distended with need as he lowered her back against the pillows and moved on to her.

'No,' he groaned, seeking her mouth, his face agonised. 'No, I can't leave you tonight.'

They made love with a ferocity that hurt, driven by despair, made savage by the knowledge that this was all they would have, this one night, and they left marks on each other with the violence of their passion.

Cadence pleaded and taunted in turn, but Jon continued to deny her, but he couldn't deny her his body and they drove each other to a bitter, excruciating pitch of shuddering ecstasy at the culmination of which their energy rebounded on them in a last agonisingly exquisite paroxysm and they collapsed, still joined, fighting for breath and no happier than they had been before.

But their energy was only temporarily spent and it happened a third time later when dawn was already paling the Indian sky outside, although the lamp still burned in the beautiful room which had become their entire world for this one night.

'Why do I have to pay the price for your distorted loyalty?' she demanded furiously, driven by the knowledge that Jon would leave her soon, that this was the last time his teeth would tug and his tongue voluptuously circle her turgid, inflamed nipples; the last time he would cause that burning flush to spread all over her body.

He raised his head to look at her, his face contorted with desire and anger. 'Because you love me,' he grated savagely, brutally, and her panted retort changed to a moan of desire as his fingers at the top of her thighs probed the most intimate hollows and recesses of her body.

A spasm of wanting shook her, making her cry out urgently as the hot melting ache in her loins became a fierce, clamorous urge, devouring her. Jon slid into her and she gripped him angrily, groaning softly and hoarsely as the deep internal shudder began in response to his tumultuous possession. She was consumed, brilliantly taken, owned, by him, so wildly out of control that he had to hold her down.

'I love you, I love you,' she gasped despairingly, and he groaned harshly, also losing all control now as they were both finally convulsed with ecstasy, filling her, pleasuring her so intensely that it felt as if the earth moved, leaving her faint, shaken and sated, but still bitterly unhappy. She tried desperately to keep him with her, but he moved away, lying beside her only for as long as it took him to steady his breathing before rising wearily from the bed, gathering his clothes and going into her bathroom.

Cadence too was weary, tender after the unaccustomed intimacy. There was an ache in the small of her back, her lips were bruised and swollen from Jon's kisses and her nipples still sensitive and rosy, but she was conscious only of the anguish that had its core in the region of her heart and spread through all her being. Her mind too was saturated with a sense of tragedy which was partly for herself but also for Jon because, knowing him, loving him, she knew the difficulty he would have in forgiving himself for this night's events.

He was dressed when he returned to the bedroom, his hair damp from a quick shower. He switched off the lamp and came to stand beside the low bed, a dark brooding figure in the grey morning light that filtered into the room.

Cadence sat up stiffly. 'Must it be this way, Jon?' she whispered.

'I'm sorry.' He was harsh yet genuinely regretful. 'I've stolen these hours from Christopher, and I can't take anything more. As it is, I don't know how I'm going to live with myself.'

'And how are you going to live without me?' Cadence retorted, growing angry again.

She saw by his face that the question had already begun to haunt him.

'Somehow I'll have to,' he stated grimly.

'How?' she challenged. 'It won't go away, will it, Jon? It will always be there, no matter how often we make love; it will always come back; it can never be finally and permanently satisfied, only temporarily.'

'Damn you! When you and Christopher leave——'

'When Christopher and I leave here, it won't get any better! You'll still think about me, you'll still want me, and I'll still love you.'

'Are you trying to put a curse on me?' he snapped.

'I'm telling you the truth and you know it.'

'Cadence, for pity's sake!'

'Where's your pity? For me?' She stopped, startled by the ear-splitting early morning voice of one of the peacocks outside, and then she began to laugh, distressingly, with a touch of hysteria. 'It should be a cock crowing, shouldn't it, Jon? It was three times, wasn't it?'

'Shut up!' Jon snapped furiously, but she couldn't help herself.

'But think of this, Jon! There've been greater wrongs done in the history of the world than tonight's, and they've been forgiven. And Christopher is a wonderful person. He would forgive us——'

'I don't want his forgiveness! Cadence, stop it!'

'And here's something else to think about,' she spat. 'While you're saving your soul or proving your loyalty to the Iversons or whatever, you're still committing a betrayal . . . a denial. Of me! I love you, Jon.'

'Cady . . .'

He moved towards her, but she put out a hand to stop him.

'Don't touch me, Jon!' She laughed again, wildly. 'I'll probably go mad and bite you. Get out, go away— now! You don't deserve me, you're not ready for me.'

He looked at her white face, her eyes burning feverishly, and then without a word, he turned and left, closing the door with a sharp click.

Cadence lay back painfully, still with a tendency to laugh. It had been such a stupid thing to say, telling him he wasn't ready for her, when he had already had her.

After a while, she sobered, but she stayed angry, discovering that it was possible to both love and hate someone at the same time.

She stayed furious for two days, sustained and strengthened by her anger although its object was absent.

Jon had gone to Delhi for a couple of days, Padmini had told her when she had finally emerged from her room that morning. She didn't know why, she said; it had been a sudden decision.

'Jaydev thinks he's cracking up,' she had added, and at that stage Cadence was still angry enough to laugh and think it served him right.

He and Christopher came back on the same day. It was also the day on which Cadence received a letter from Stephanie Iverson, an ordinary, friendly letter, but there had been a postscript enquiring if anything was wrong 'out there'. Why hadn't she heard from Cadence and why had Christopher's only letter omitted all mention of her? She hoped nothing serious was wrong.

It awoke the guilt Cadence had failed to experience after she and Joh had made love, and Christopher's return from Kashmir compounded it. She was swept by shame as she looked at him, thinking he looked tired and strained although he had told her his trip had been free of problems. There was a constraint between them, she realised, and she didn't know if she alone was responsible for it or if Christopher too had something on his mind.

She wanted to tell him, to confess what had happened and tell him how she felt; she wanted to ask him to release her from their engagement, but she couldn't risk it when she didn't know the full extent of the effect such an action would have on Jon——her beloved Jon whose eyes had asked that urgent question of her when he had arrived at the palace just a couple of hours after Christopher's return. She had looked back at him, silently reassuring, and although he had relaxed a little, his countenance had remained dark and taut, all stark angles or shadowed hollows, and his mouth had stayed harsh and grim.

Constraint lay on them all these days, including poor Jahanara, yearning after Christopher, pining for him. Only when they were in the company of the Nayars or their children did the tension abate a little; otherwise it seemed set to continue without relief. But how much more could any of them take? Cadence wondered bleakly, watching Jon suffering as she was, loving him and yet unable to do anything to help him, to ease him. He never came near her, and she knew his frustration matched hers.

And what was wrong with Christopher? Did he know, did he guess? There was definitely something . . .

Once, searching desperately for whatever vestige of hope she could find to cling to in order not to lose her mind entirely, Cadence said to Christopher, 'It's probably not fair of me to tell you, but Jahanara is in love with you. Did you know?'

'Yes, I know, but I've tried not to show that I do. I don't want to embarrass her.'

His fair face was so calm, his eyes so clear and serene, that she knew, as she had always known really, that she couldn't look to Jahanara for an easy solution.

'Poor Jahanara,' she murmured, a world of sadness in her voice, and he looked at her curiously.

'Why did you mention it?' he asked quietly.

Cadence's expression grew hunted and she couldn't quite meet his eyes. 'Oh, I don't know. A whim, I suppose. Christo, isn't it time were were planning the rest of our time here? What about the Taj, and Delhi?

And you said you'd probably be going to Kashmir again and I could go with you.'

'Yes, we must think about it,' he agreed, accepting the change of subject without question, and laughing a little. 'The truth is, I'm lazy. I don't want to stir.'

Another time it was he who introduced a subject that disturbed her as they sat out in the warm darkness of an October night after the Nayars and Jon had retreated indoors, making the mosquitoes their excuse.

'How are you and Jon getting on these days?' he asked casually, and Cadence was glad of the darkness because she knew she had assumed a guilty expression, her cheeks flushed, her mouth trembling.

'Oh, fair to middling,' she offered flippantly, but then because it mattered so much, she asked seriously, 'Christo, you and your parents have never talked as if you feel Jon owes you anything, you simply love him, so why does he seem to have this idea that he's terrifically in your debt?'

'Oh, that? I've always known he had this obsession, though he never talks about it. I don't think my parents realise . . .' Christopher paused thoughtfully. 'It's crazy, needless to say. If we gave him anything of value, he gave us as much, and I don't happen to think those things have a price on them . . . But Jon is—Jon! When he makes up his mind about anything, it takes something cataclysmic to make him change it. That's just the way he is.'

'But what does he imagine would have happened to him without you people?'

'Cadence . . .' Christopher hesitated. 'I don't know, love, not specifically. He's not one for baring his soul, you know, but perhaps that's it—his soul. Look, he had a horrific childhood, seeing his mother killed, losing his father and then taking off the way he did, losing himself for months. I think he'd lost all a child's innocence by the time he came to us. He was hardly human, a frozen shell without a soul, or with only the dark side of the soul left, hard and incapable of emotion . . . And for some reason, we were . . . like an antidote. He thawed, some of the damage was reversed, though I still see that dark side occasionally. I don't know why it was that we had that influence on him.'

'You're good, you and your parents, intrinsically good without even being conscious of it,' she murmured. 'That's why.'

'But listen, Cadence!' Suddenly Christopher was speaking urgently. 'It was nothing we did or gave deliberately, we made no effort or sacrifices, and Jon's a strong enough personality to have got himself back together eventually without us. You've got to understand that!'

She wondered what made him so insistent and was again grateful for the darkness that hid her face, but she was still too habitually candid and confiding not to sigh her thoughts aloud: 'I think it's Jon who has got to understand that.'

'Yes. Perhaps one day he will.'

Christopher also sighed. For his friend, or for some other reason? Cadence was beginning to feel afraid now. Did he know? She couldn't ask, in case he didn't. When he kissed her good night a little later, he did so lingeringly, gently, parting from her silently, and shame swept over her once more.

He was, as she had observed, a genuinely good person, and he loved her so much. Without any of the sense of obligation Jon felt, she could nonetheless share to a great extent in his guilt at their betrayal of such a man. She ought to love Christopher, she thought, and she would have done if only love could have made its choices on pure merit. Instead it was the

most wayward of all emotions, and she loved that
other darkly complex man with all those flaws and
problems that made loving him so painful.

Jon! This was yet another night when Cadence
went sleepless, her mind, heart and body all
tormented as thoughts, memories, of that dark lover
of one night only possessed her. She understood
Jon's feelings; it was inevitable that such a man as
he was, once he gave his loyalty or felt himself
under an obligation, would never waver from his
commitment; and she also understood how the
Iversons' gift of love must have always seemed to
him, the light that had pierced his darkness long ago
and remained bright and constant ever since—but
dear God, this situation was doing none of them any
good.

It certainly wasn't doing her any good, she was
thinking the following evening, arrested by the sight of
herself in her dressing-table mirror. She stared at her
figure, assessing the evidence of loss of weight, and at
her face, noting the smudgy shadows under her eyes,
the deepening hollows beneath her cheeks, and as for
her eyes and mouth——! She remembered a confident
smile and clear eyes, and look at them now! How could
he do this to her when——

Transfixed, she stared at herself for a few frozen
moments, before whirling and striding out of her room
again, although her intention to shower and change for
the evening remained unfulfilled. She sped along the
corridor and down the magnificent flight of stairs,
almost at a run.

She knew where Jon was. She always did these days.
She flew into the study he used, noting that Jahanara
was absent, but it wouldn't have mattered if she had
still been at work.

'Cady?' Jon stood up, startled.

'Jon, I've had enough,' announced Cadence, coming to a halt at his desk.

'So have I, believe me,' he countered with grim humour.

'No, look! Look at me—my face! Look at this!' She pulled at the waistband of her shorts that were a colour somewhere between lemon and lime and her favourite pair for emphasising her tan. 'I'm losing weight. I never really thought it happened, but it does! I'm fading away! What are you smiling at? How can you do this to me?'

'Cadence, you know——'

'How can you do this when you love me?'

'When I——' Jon had gone white. 'How did you know?' he asked numbly.

'I'm not sure, I just do.' She paused before continuing more calmly. 'I suppose I've known a long time in one way. I'd say in my mind—he doesn't love me—but it never seemed to matter, so I think I must have known, inside myself, somehow.'

'And I suppose there's no point in my denying it?' he challenged sardonically, beginning to recover from his shock.

'None.' Cadence smiled tauntingly.

Jon expelled his breath resignedly. 'I've loved you and known I loved you since the day we met in Bombay. It began at the airport, with wanting you, and by the time we sat in that coffee shop . . . When I heard you answering me, saying yes, you loved Christopher—that's when I knew. I wanted it to be me you loved, and later it was, and there wasn't a bloody thing I could do.'

'You couldn't even tell me,' she accused sadly. 'So long, Jon, and you never told me.'

'I knew if I did that you'd never leave me alone, that you'd be quite merciless—and I was right,' he added tiredly. 'Because here you are.'

'I'm fighting for my life, Jon,' she declared passionately. 'For my happiness and for yours. How can you do this to me? How can you do it to yourself? Look at you! Jon darling, I can't bear it!'

'You have to! We both have to!' The blue eyes flashed defiantly.

'You fool! We were made for each other.'

'That's the irony of it,' he agreed savagely.

'Jon?' Cadence's voice had softened again. 'Please, won't you tell Christo?'

'No!'

'Or let me tell him?'

'No!' His refusal was violent.

'Darling . . ' She hesitated, wavering between rage and despair, raving and weeping. 'Jon darling, we know the Iversons, the people they are. They love you, that's all. They wouldn't want you to make this sort of sacrifice.'

'They wouldn't want it, they wouldn't ask it—that's why I owe it to them,' Jon returned in a blistering tone. 'Cadence, can't you understand? How can I live with you, be with you, be happy with you . . . knowing that Christopher Iverson loves you?'

'Jon . . .' She made a hopeless gesture with her hands.

'Can you deny that he loves you?' Jon pressed.

'No. No, I can't deny it,' she conceded reluctantly. 'But what about us? You and me?'

'Cadence, I know!'

He came round the end of the desk, reaching for her, and Cadence collapsed into his arms, shaking.

'It's so difficult,' she muttered against his shoulder, sliding her arms about him.

'Oh, God, I know!' he repeated against her bright hair, shaking as violently as she was, his arms tightening convulsively. 'It's killing me, seeing you so unhappy and knowing I'm doing that to you, subduing all that brilliant vitality, stopping your lovely laughter . . . I love you, and I'm hurting you.'

'And sometimes I'm angry and hate you for it,' she told him honestly. 'But that part is always superficial. I love you, Jon, and I do understand.'

'Yes.'

They stood there, holding each other, desire stirring, but despair was stronger still now. They were essentially two unhappy people, trying to comfort each other in a hopeless situation.

Cadence remembered what she had said to him as he had left her after their one night of love. She had told him he wasn't ready for her, and the words had come from her subconscious understanding of the truth. He loved her, but he wasn't ready for her because he had yet to free himself from the other obsession that ruled him. Again it was the difference between men and women; the former with their divided loyalties, while women were the single-minded sex.

She was beginning to believe it was a difference that could never be reconciled.

CHAPTER TEN

THEY were approaching a breaking point of another kind, Cadence reflected fretfully a few evenings later, sitting in the palace garden with Jon and Christopher. Jaydev and Padmini had excused themselves a few minutes earlier, and with their departure the terrible tension had returned. In another few minutes, she knew, Jon too would drift away. He never stayed long with her and Christopher.

She glanced surreptitiously at the two men, dark and fair. The gentle evening darkness allowed no colours save black and white and grey, and she was seeing them with her mind rather than her eyes, because she was aware of the colours of eyes and skin and clothes.

A vast aching hunger welled up in her as she looked at Jon, an engulfing emotional hunger made physical by her need to express all the prodigious, endless, extravagant love he forced her to contain, refusing to receive it. She ached, unendurably, to release it, to pour it over him, lavishly, wantonly, until he drowned ecstatically in its richness . . .

And he would not have it. He denied her an outlet, and the mounting pressure built and built as the days went by, becoming intolerable. Already it seeped from her, in little ways, the gathering excess of love she tried to hold back. Love was in the way she looked at him, the way she spoke to him . . .

Jon saw and heard, and she knew he was disturbed, watchful and guarded, because surely Christopher too must see and hear. She was no actress. Not even her care and concern for Jon could make her one.

She kept trying, though, because he demanded it, and now she hastily lowered her eyes to where her hands lay on her lap, slender fingers taut against the patterned oyster silk of the sari she had finally been persuaded to wear, although she knew she could never do the justice Indian women did to this most graceful of garments. She stared at her hands, wondering absently where the light came from that was caught in the diamonds of her ring. Not starlight, surely, although it was a bright night.

She had no right to be wearing it, she thought savagely, twisting it round and round. Its presence on her finger cheated all three of them.

The silence of her companions had a disturbing quality, suddenly, and she raised her eyes to find them both watching her hands, watching her traitor fingers wrestling with that ill-placed ring. Instantly, guiltily, she forced their stillness, and was grateful for the casual way Jon broke the silence:

'Have you two made any decision about Delhi and the other places on your itinerary yet?'

'Not specifically,' Christopher replied easily. 'There's still plenty of time and, as I told Cadence recently, I'm lazy. Will you be joining us when we do decide, Jon?'

'Sorry,' Jon answered expressionlessly. 'I'm working again, but I'll give Jahanara a day or two off whenever you decide to go to Agra, if she and Hanif would like to accompany you.'

Another silence fell, as if the two men had spent their last strength on that small exchange, and Cadence wanted to scream. She knew Jon was anxious for her and Christopher to be away from the palace as much as possible, but Christopher had been oddly reluctant to discuss their planned trips, evading all her own attempts to exert pressure. In fact, he had been altogether strangely elusive lately, going out on his own almost daily, and for the first time she wondered what was behind it. Until now, she had been so preoccupied with her own unhappiness and Jon's growing frustration that she had dismissed Christopher's disappearances almost unthinkingly, assuming that he was running checks on more hotels or making further assessments of Sashi, Sunila and Iverson Travel's other Rajasthan guides.

Abruptly, his voice startling as it fell into the strained silence, Christopher asked, 'What's wrong with you two?'

Cadence's head jerked upward. Her heart was thudding painfully and she couldn't look at Jon. Why didn't he answer? Why did he leave the lying to her? He knew how unconvincing she was. She felt faint and dizzy, frantically trying to summon words, plausible words, so that she wouldn't have to let Jon down; her nails dug into her palms, she was hyperventilating and the gripping agony in her heart was spreading through all her being.

From a great distance, she heard her own voice, quick and breathless, saying, 'Christo, Christopher dear, do you know?'

Had she really said it? She must have, because suddenly Jon stood beside her chair although she hadn't seen him move. She sat paralysed, expecting to feel his hands at her throat, strangling her, but instead it was her shoulder that he touched, his fingers warm and strong and unexpectedly reassuring.

'No, Cadence.' There was pain in his voice, and a quiet authority. 'I've inflicted enough suffering on you already. If I let you take this on as well, I'll never be able to look at you again. Let me tell him.'

'You don't have to, either of you,' Christopher said quietly, standing up. 'I do know. I've known for a long time. I first suspected something that day we went to Amber, and gradually I've become more and more convinced. You're neither of you very good at dissembling ... That's why I went to Kashmir alone, to try and come to terms with it. I didn't say anything because I was waiting for you—to be ready to tell me. But you don't have to ... to be explicit. I know.'

'Christopher——' Jon's fingers bit painfully into Cadence's shoulder.

Christopher gave an odd angry laugh. 'I had it all planned, I was going to make it easy for you! I was going to say, well, I'm relieved, because you see, Jahanara Khan and I have fallen in love ... I got the idea from Cadence! But it's not true. I can't lie, not to you two. Nevertheless, it is ... all right.'

'You're still lying, Christopher,' Jon accused harshly.

'Yes, I am! No, it's not all right!' Horrified, Cadence saw that Christopher's eyes glittered with something that wasn't starshine. 'I'm devastated, I'm sick and sad and sore—but what the hell can I do? I couldn't be happy with Cadence now, so the next best thing is for the two of you to be happy together.'

Jon had withdrawn his hand from Cadence's shoulder, and she had stood up quietly. She had no place or business here.

'Christopher, I'm sorry,' she whispered. 'Jon.'

His face was a mask; only his eyes spoke of his anguish. She touched his hand and went away, and they let her. It was between the two of them. She was simply the girl who had caused the conflict, the catalyst, finally unimportant as the consequences came to be considered.

A smile of self-mockery curved her mouth as she went inside, hearing the murmur of their voices behind her, but when she reached her room she wept long and bitterly for what she had done to the two men she loved, one as a lover and the other as a friend.

For once she slept, worn out by the unaccustomed storm of tears, but she was up early. No one else seemed to be about apart from the inevitable squad of servants, and since she had no heart for anything, swimming or walking, she yielded to their attempts to persuade her to breakfast on the verandah, although she wasn't hungry either.

It was here that Christopher joined her, and she looked at him uncertainly as he sat down. His expression was calm, his eyes a little sad, but he was smiling at her.

'It's all right, Cady, don't say anything.' He sighed, pouring himself a glass of mango juice. 'It was inevitable, I suspect. The two of you . . . all that fire and energy. You could have been made for each other.'

'Christo.' She swallowed. 'You're making it easier than I deserve.'

'Jon says you haven't had it easy at all.'

Her mouth shook. 'Will you . . . take this back?'

He looked at the ring she had pulled off, a profound regret in his eyes. 'I'd have said, keep it, especially as it was designed for you, but you'll be happier returning it, won't you?'

'Yes,' she whispered as he took it from her and dropped it into his shirt pocket. 'Christo, your parents?'

'I think I must be the one to explain to them,' he said slowly. 'They'll understand, but you and Jon are so busy feeling guilty at the moment, they'll think you've really got something to be guilty about.'

'We have.'

'Oh, no! You couldn't have helped yourselves. If

you could, it wouldn't have happened. I know, and my parents know, how much you both care about me.'

'Ah, God, do you know how . . . how you're making me feel?' Cadence gulped. 'Jon said once that . . . that good people can destroy, with their goodness and their kindness. I know what he meant.'

'Yes.' Christopher laughed suddenly. 'He wanted me to hit him, I wished I could, it would have made him feel better, but I couldn't . . . It's just the way I am. I can't help it. Listen, Cady, you've got to stop feeling guilty and so has Jon. It will be harder for him, I think. I'm not being noble or anything. I really do want you to be happy.'

'And how will you be happy? That's what will haunt Jon,' she said sadly.

'That was something I wanted to discuss with you. I'll always love you, Cady, I can't lie about that. I didn't want to lose you, but I can't spend the rest of my life mourning you like some idiot in a poem . . . I want a wife and children.' He paused as if wondering how to go on. 'I hope all this doesn't sound too cynical, but I've thought it out carefully. I mentioned last night that I'd been going to tell you that lie about Jahanara and then couldn't go through with it. But it's not totally a lie. Some of the times I've been out on my own recently, I've been visiting Jahanara and Hanif. I couldn't go through with the lie last night, but . . . she loves me, I find her physically attractive, and I like and respect her enough to be fond of her. What do you think? Is it fair to her?'

Cadence thought about it a while. 'It's fair if you tell her the truth, Christo. Hanif needn't know, but she must be aware of what it is you're offering her and decide for herself if she can settle for less than equal loving. I've found out, we've all found out, in recent weeks, how much misery lying can cause. It's just not worth it, even to be kind. But Christo, will it be for yourself? You're not planning this to be kind to her, or to Jon and me, or to your parents?'

'It's for me,' he confirmed seriously. 'It won't be what I'd hoped to have with you, it couldn't be, whoever I chose, I'm afraid, but as I say, I do want a family, and she's a gentle and loving girl.'

'It won't be easy,' she warned, her heart aching for the imperfection of the future he and Jahanara would face if it worked out. 'There'll be problems, resentment . . . perhaps on both sides. But I think she might accept it. She loves you and . . . that's how women are. We don't have too much pride when we love. I'd still want to share Jon's life, even if he couldn't love me.'

He looked sad, saw her look of contrition and made an effort to smile. 'I'll get used to it. But for pity's sake—no, for my sake, make sure the two of you are happy.'

'But can we be?' Doubt darkened her eyes. 'Will you and Jon still be friends, Christopher? We can't ask it of you, but without that, Jon will never be able to live happily with me.'

He looked down at the table in silence for a few seconds before speaking gently.

'Cadence, you were there to begin with last night, you were there when he finally got his priorities right and refused to let you assume the burden of telling me. Yes, love, Jon and I will still be friends.'

'It can never be the same, though, can it?'

'No. He knows that. He's an adult man and he knows, just as I do, and you do, and you say Jahanara does, that . . . no one can have it all.'

'Last night . . . Was he very upset?' Cadence's voice shook. 'I haven't seen him.'

'He's gone.'

'Gone?' She was dead white.

'To Delhi, I think. Cady, don't!'

She was crying. 'How could he?'

'He said you'd understand.'

'I understand!' she wept, violently. 'He's angry, he can't forgive me—he warned me once! I let him down by saying what I did last night, and forcing him to tell you, and . . . oh, Christopher, it's all been for nothing, you and him and me, all of us being so unhappy—for nothing!'

Christopher looked troubled. 'Cady, didn't you listen to me just now? I said he finally got his priorities right last night. You know how much he loves you. He'll be back, but you've got to give him time, time to think things through, to adjust . . . He's still hating himself pretty badly just now. It's himself he has to forgive, and he will do, believe me. He's too intelligent not to, ultimately. He won't let it . . . all be for nothing, as you put it.'

'No!'

This final denial of happiness by Jon was too much for her in her overwrought state, worn out by the strain of recent weeks. She could only interpret it as a bitter rejection, punishing her for her unthinking words to Christopher last night. She had failed Jon, and he would not forgive her.

'Cadence, yes!' Christopher put a hand over hers. 'Listen to me, love. Jon told me things last night that I don't have the right to repeat to you. They're for him to say to you, some day when you're alone, but some of them you know already, or you would know if you were thinking clearly . . . But you're not, are you, poor darling? You've had a rough time and you're at the end of your tether. But please, be patient, give him time, because in some ways it's been even harder on him. Another thing he told me about was the hell it's been, believing he was wronging two people, you and me ... Jon is very hard on himself when he fails to live up to the personal standards he sets himself, and those are impossibly high for some reason.'

'The Iverson influence,' she murmured, beginning to calm down.

Christopher looked rueful. 'You ought to hate us. Without that sense of obligation Jon felt towards us, this whole thing would have been a lot less complicated and painful.'

'I ought to, yes, but I don't. After all, it wasn't deliberate, just the way Jon's particular personality reacted to the particular virtue in your family.' Cadence managed a smile. 'I'm not going to go looking for Jon; he must come to me. I'll give him five days. After that I'm going home—and right now I'm going to my room to fix my face before Jaydev and Padmini arrive and find me looking like this. Thank you, Christopher, thank you ... for everything.'

He watched her go, imagining the life she and Jon would make together if they ever managed to get things sorted out. Two such strong and vitally energetic personalities would inevitably produce plenty of drama. There might be conflict and even dark tragedy, but Cadence's capacity for happiness, dulled of late, would revive and turn tragedy to triumph; but they would certainly also touch the heights, and that was what he envied them—more specifically, it was what he envied Jon, although he knew now that he could never have as fully awoken her woman's love as Jon had. He accepted that already, and one day the acceptance would feel more comfortable than it did at present.

He just hoped Jon made it back in the five days Cadence had stipulated.

It took three days, during which Cadence swung

between faint hope and a deep despair. She wanted to believe Christopher, and sometimes she did, because the one thing she remained sure of was Jon's love for her. But could he forgive her, could he live with her? Who could predict the reactions of so moody and obsessive a man? Not even the woman who loved and understood him . . . .

She seemed to have lost all her optimism, all her tendency to think positively. She had come to the end of her endurance. The unhappiness and dishonesty of past weeks had disagreed with her as violently as a poison. The lying had stopped, but it was as if a residue still remained in her system, leaving her ashamed and depressed.

She was also embarrassed. Jaydev and Padmini had been tactful about the broken engagement, but they must wonder why she remained here at the palace with no apparent reason for doing so—unless Christopher had told them she was waiting for Jon—instead of decently going away and giving Christopher a chance to get over her, forget her, in peace.

Not that they saw much of Christopher. He had already begun his courtship of Jahanara Khan, and it was taking place away from the palace. Somehow Hanif had been satisfied that his sister was in no way directly responsible for the broken engagement and, at the same time, reassured as to Christopher's motivation and intentions.

So, in a sense, the dishonesty continued, Cadence thought sadly. This time it was Hanif Khan who was being deceived. She had learnt this during the course of the awkward conversation Jahanara had sought with her. They had both been ill at ease, afraid of offending or embarrassing each other, an altogether uncomfortable fifteen minutes.

'My brother would be angry and offended by the

full truth,' Jahanara had explained at one stage. 'He would think Christopher was insulting me and that I was demeaning myself by disregarding the insult. Things are black or white, right or wrong, to Hanif, though he has made one compromise in that Christopher is outside of Islam . . . for my sake he has agreed that we may see each other. But if he knew that it was—on the rebound . . .' Jahanara shook her head and the dark plait she wore swung gently. 'I don't know myself if I can handle it. I'll need time to consider . . . I should hate you, Cadence. I do resent you.'

'That's natural.'

'But bad. Bad for my peace of mind, and for Christopher. If I decide . . . I'll have to get over it if we're to have a relationship. I must learn to rationalise, but it's hard when the emotions are involved. You can't help being the woman Christopher loves any more than he can help being the man I love.'

'Jahanara, I'm sorry.' Cadence was nearly in tears—she was always weepy these days. 'I wish I'd known long ago what I know now and been saved from making the mistake of becoming engaged to him, letting him . . . letting him——'

'Letting him become accustomed to the idea that you were part of his future,' Jahanara supplied sadly, resentfully.

There was nothing more to be said and they parted as constrainedly as they had met. Cadence thought Jahanara would eventually marry Christopher and, she hoped, be happy. Christopher would be a good husband and Jahanara would probably settle for what he was offering rather than lose him to bachelorhood or another girl. She was feminine and loving and in time she might make herself indispensable to him.

Cadence's thoughts switched to Jon again. When would he return? Would he return?

He did, one afternoon, startling her as she sat on a cushioned outdoor chair beside the swimming pool, her tanned skin warm from the sun, its rich colour emphasised by her saffron and white bikini. A jug of lime juice and a glass stood on the table beside her, and she was trying to lose herself in the *Times of India*. She was alone; Christopher and Jaydev were out, small Anjuna was asleep and Padmini had gone with one of the chauffeurs to fetch Pratap from school.

She hadn't heard him coming, so she was unprepared when she looked up from the paper and saw him standing there in jeans and a short-sleeved cream shirt, watching her expressionlessly. Her heart seemed to leap to her throat, settle again and start pounding furiously, and she knew she had gone pale.

'Jon.' Her eyes were dark with apprehension and uncertainty.

'Cadence,' he acknowledged in the same tone. 'You waited.'

She couldn't tell what he was thinking, standing there in the sunshine, magnificently male, infinitely beloved. Oh, God, she thought frantically, she loved him beyond life, and if she had lost him——

'Jon,' she repeated, urgently now as she dropped the paper and stood up. 'Don't look at me like that. I know you must hate me for saying what I did, forcing you into the position where you had to tell Christopher, and I'm sorry . . . I'm so sorry! I let you down, I failed you, and I can't bear it if you——'

'Cadence!' Jon interrupted, coming to her but not touching her. 'What are you talking about?'

'And coming between you and Christopher!' She had begun to cry. 'Causing you both so much unhappiness. I hate myself, but I didn't, I never . . .'

'Darling, no!' He pulled her into his arms then and she felt his body tense, a solid support for her weak, shuddering frame. 'What is all this? I came here to ask, to beg your forgiveness, and instead it's you apologising . . . It's because I went away, isn't it? Ah, dear God, is there no end to the unhappiness I cause other people? Cadence, Cady, don't cry, please don't, my dear love, I can't bear it. You're meant to be strong and happy . . . Darling, you've done nothing, except be yourself. It's me! I can't do anything right!'

His words took a few moments to register, then suddenly Cadence was laughing through her tears, sliding her arms about him and holding him very tight.

'We none of us can if we keep measuring ourselves against the Iversons. We've made a mess of things, truly, but now?' She looked up into his taut face. 'Now it's all right, Jon, isn't it? You and me?'

'It's all right . . . only if you say so,' he said slowly, strangely hesitant. 'Oh, God, Cadence! I can't believe how stupid and cruel I've been, and I don't know how you can forgive me. The way I made you suffer . . . forcing you to live a lie, using your love to make you do so. That's manipulation. How can you love such a bastard?'

'Easily. Oh, Jon darling, don't!' She couldn't bear the self-hatred she saw in his eyes. 'Kiss me, Jon, quickly!'

'I can't, not yet!' His mouth twisted. 'And you standing half naked in my arms too! Cadence, do you understand? I failed you so badly, but not because I didn't love you. I loved you more . . . more than I dreamed I could ever love, and that's what I couldn't accept. God, if I'd ever thought about it, I should have guessed that somewhere, some time, there'd be someone I'd love this way, but I never did. I suppose

I assumed that even if I loved a woman she'd be second to the Iversons, because of their influence on my life, because of what they'd done for me. Then this hit me ... You, Cadence! And I couldn't handle it, I refused to accept it. I thought I had to love them more, I thought I must. I didn't want to let you replace them ... and that's why I failed you so badly. I should have put you first instead of my loyalty to them, but I couldn't. For a long time, I couldn't. It was only after that night we spent together that I slowly started to realise, still fighting it, that I'd rather hurt them than you ... I don't know if your words to Christopher precipitated my acceptance of the fact that you are the most important person in my life, but I'd like you to believe that it would have come anyway, if not that night, then the next day or the day after ... You looked so unhappy that night, sitting there twisting your ring, and I felt like a monster. You're not wearing it now.'

'No.' His embrace had slackened and she showed him her left hand, smiling into his eyes. 'Now, will you kiss me? Oh, Jon, these last three days have been worse than anything that went before, not knowing what you were thinking or feeling, whether you were angry——'

'That's another thing I couldn't get right,' he said regretfully, his dark face serious. 'What a fool, what a crazy fool ... I finally realise that you matter more to me than anyone else in the world and that I'll suffer anything rather than let you be hurt, so I promptly leave you without a word of reassurance ... In Delhi, I realised what I'd done, how you must be feeling, so I came rushing back today. I'm sorry, Cadence.'

'Jon, Jon, it's all right, darling, stop hating yourself. I love you.' She covered his throat and jaw with a flurry of soft, urgent kisses and his arms tightened about her. 'Christopher told me you had said I would understand why you had to go, and in a way I did, but . . . Oh, I don't know! All the lying, and wanting you so badly . . . they must have got to me. It's over now, but never, ever, leave me again!'

'Darling! Oh, God, Cadence!' Jon was incoherent, his hands stroking her hair, pushing it back from her face, his mouth touching her temple, her cheek, her jaw, making her tremble with longing. 'You're incredible—wonderful! The most wonderful woman in the world.'

'I don't think that's really true, but I hope you always think it is!' She laughed, lyrically, because the shadows were receding and she could see the future, gloriously bright and beautiful.

'And I don't know how you can love me,' he added. 'You could have anyone.'

'So I picked the best, naturally! What's a wonderful girl like me doing with a man like you? You must be wonderful too, Jon, the most wonderful man in the world.'

'I don't feel it!' But he was starting to smile at her nonsense.

'You will,' she promised. 'Oh, you will, darling—darling!'

Then their mouths met, fused, and they clung to each other, swaying together, and joy leapt in them for this first kiss to be shared in freedom from shame and guilt, stolen from no one, a promise, a pledge and a right.

Bombay's airport was as chaotic in December as it had been on that early September morning when Fate had caught up with Jon and Cadence.

Cadence looked at Jon as they waited—her husband, but that was their secret, shared with no one, because they were to have a second wedding at home later, for Cadence's family's sake. It had happened in a Christian church in Delhi, and their long, ecstatic honeymoon had been an introduction to Jon's India, following the route of his boyhood adventure and learning of all that had happened to him then, horrific and funny and terrifying and beautiful.

Meanwhile, Christopher and Jahanara's relationship had progressed rapidly. Their engagement had been announced and they had flown to England, accompanied by Hanif, to introduce Jahanara to her future parents-in-law and country. Hanif had returned after a week, all the time he could spare from business, and Jon and Cadence had gone back to Rajasthan for a few days to hear from him that he was reassured about Jahanara's future, that Aubrey and Stephanie were thrilled with her and that Christopher and Jahanara themselves seemed perfectly happy.

They were to be married in India in January, and Aubrey and Stephanie would be accompanying them when they arrived in December to prepare.

Which was why they were here at the airport, waiting. Cadence looked at Jon again as he stood talking to Hanif Khan. This was the real test, she knew, but she only felt slightly nervous. In the last deliriously happy weeks, she had seen the complete restoration of his self-respect. He had stopped hating himself, and she knew the joy they found in their relationship was responsible, because how could he doubt that finally they had followed the right course? They lived for each other, and their shared love, a matchless compound of passion, tenderness, caring and laughter, had already made up for the agony they had endured to win it.

The first passengers were beginning to stream through, and Jon turned to find Cadence, smiling and holding out an arm as their eyes met. She smiled back, moving to stand at his side, slipping an arm about his waist at the same moment as his arm curled about her shoulders. She leaned against him, reading his mood from the absence of tension in his body, its familiar, beloved warmth reaching her through the material of the punjabi she wore, reassuring her as always.

Then suddenly there they were, Jahanara and Stephanie first, followed by Christopher and Aubrey, and Jon and Cadence were separated in the confusion of greetings. Cadence had her own small ordeal to face; she was relieved when Jahanara turned to her immediately after greeting Hanif, smiling happily and embracing her like an old friend, but it was darling Stephanie who had caused her anxiety.

'Dear Cadence!' Stephanie hugged her and then stood back to look at her. 'You're so brown! Darling, I'm so glad you're still going to be joining the family, through Jon . . . Oh, Jon dear!'

He had heard, Cadence realised happily as he bent to kiss Stephanie. She had missed his reunion with Christopher, but he was wholly at ease, so it must be all right. And here was Christopher . . .

'Happy, Cady?' he asked her quietly, brushing her cheek with his lips.

'Very happy, Christo,' she assured him warmly, smiling at Jon who was smiling at her, with Christopher smiling at them both, and for a few seconds they were a triangle again, but a happier one than before, with the lies and the pain dissolved. Only for a few seconds, because here was Aubrey Iverson, greeting her, greeting Jon . . .

A few minutes later, having fought their way outside, Cadence and Stephanie reached one of the two cars they were using. Pausing, they looked back for the others. Aubrey was there with Hanif and

Jahanara, and bringing up the rear were Jon and Christopher, engaged in some exchange which ended in mutual laughter. Cadence and Stephanie looked at each other with perfect understanding, smiling.

It was going to be all right.

'It's going to be all right, isn't it?' Cadence said to Jon in the privacy of their hotel room that night as he joined her in bed.

'Yes.' He didn't need to ask what she meant. His hand descended gently on her swelling breast as he bent over her, his eyes alight with adoration. 'But it wouldn't matter too much if it wasn't. Nothing really matters except you . . . Only you, my darling.'

'And you, my dear love.' She smiled up at him, lovingly. 'That's why I'm glad it's going to be all right, my dear, dear love!'

Then her eyes closed as his mouth touched hers. She felt the length of his hard body all along hers, so perfectly matched that they became aroused simultaneously, and she wound her arms about him, trembling with love and joy as she yielded to the rapture they would always share.

They had earned the right to be together.

Coming Next Month

935 THE IMPOSSIBLE WOMAN Emma Darcy
A landscape gardener has designs on a celebrated Sydney architect. Only
he says he isn't interested in a lifetime commitment, and it isn't in her
nature to settle for less.

936 LONG JOURNEY BACK Robyn Donald
The man she loved jilted her in favor of a more advantageous marriage.
Now he wants her back. But why should she trust him just because he's
divorced and says he never stopped loving her?

937 PRISONER Vanessa James
The daughter of a wealthy businessman appears to be the target of an
elaborate kidnapping in Rome. Why, then, is the kidnapper so determined
to hold the young girl's companion—if it's money he's after?

938 ESCAPE FROM THE HAREM Mary Lyons
Four years ago an estranged wife was lucky to escape the desert
kingdom of Dhoman with a broken heart. Now her heart is on the line
when her husband, the new sultan demands her return—with
their daughter.

939 GLASS SLIPPERS AND UNICORNS Carole Mortimer
An easily flustered secretary succumbs to pressure when her quick-
witted boss persuades her to pose as his lover to help flush out the
saboteur of his business holdings in Florida.

940 THE LONELY SEASON Susan Napier
On an island near Fiji, the man who accused a children's book illustrator
of destroying his sister's marriage needs her help to win the love of his
deaf son. It's her chance to prove her innocence at last.

941 WIN OR LOSE Kay Thorpe
Desire was never the problem in the troubled marriage between a
journalist and a famous sportsman. Communication was. No wonder her
husband refuses to believe divorce will solve everything.

942 SHADOW PRINCESS Sophie Weston
A Paris research chemist can't understand her aristocratic cousin's
unwise love affairs—until a certain concert pianist makes her feel alive—
almost reckless—for the first time in her life.

Available in December wherever paperback books are sold, or through
Harlequin Reader Service:

In the U.S.
P.O. Box 1397
Buffalo, N.Y.
14240-1397

In Canada
P.O. Box 603
Fort Erie, Ontario
L2A 9Z9

Six exciting series
for you every month...
from Harlequin

Harlequin Romance·
The series that started it all

Tender, captivating and heartwarming...
love stories that sweep you off to faraway places
and delight you with the magic of love.

◆

Harlequin Presents·
Powerful contemporary love
stories...as individual as the
women who read them

The No. 1 romance series...
exciting love stories for you, the woman of today...
a rare blend of passion and dramatic realism.

◆

Harlequin Superromance®
It's more than romance...
it's Harlequin Superromance

A sophisticated, contemporary romance-fiction
series, providing you with a longer,
more involving read...a richer mix of complex plots,
realism and adventure.

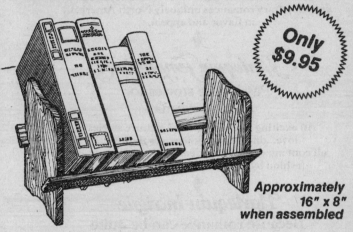